Love, Under Contract

Martin Brothers Book 1

Nina High

Nina High

ISBN-13: 9798883930576
ISBN-10: 1477123456

Cover design by:Getcovers.com
Library of Congress Control Number: 2018675309
Printed in the United States of America

Contents

Nina High

Visit subscribepage.io/6XtlP3 to join my mailing list for sneak peeks of the next books in the series and release day links.

Synopysis

Marriage proposal or business proposition?

When Charisse steps out of a job interview, she's met with an offer that blurs the lines between the boardroom and the altar. Dru Martin, a billionaire married to his job, proposes a deal rather than a romance—a marriage of convenience to fulfill family obligations.

Charisse Turner
The last thing I expected after interviewing for a job was a marriage proposal, especially from Dru Martin, the sexy Black billionaire I met the night before. But here I am, contemplating a contract that could change my life. I need the money, and Dru seems nice enough. Yet, the closer I get to Dru, the more I wonder if my heart is part of the bargain.

Dru Martin
Running an empire is easy; it's love that's complicated. So, when my mother gave me an ultimatum to settle down or forfeit the family empire, I did what any savvy businessman would do— I proposed a deal: a simple contract of marriage to Charisse, a woman intriguing enough to make this charade bearable. If we follow the plan with scheduled kisses and coordinated social media posts, we can convince everyone we're in love. But when the lines start to blur, I'm left questioning whether this arrangement is just about business, or something more.

Chapter 1

Charisse

There are just a few minutes before my planning period ends. I hate that the quiet part of my day is over, but I love that my last class comes next. Whitney Houston blasts from my Bluetooth speaker. I always start class with music, and nineties classics are safe for school. Selena was last week's flavor. Whitney's this week's.

I open my email and see that there's a response to my last application for student loan forgiveness. I'd given them every single piece of documentation I had. I know I qualify. My loans are so high because it took me six years to figure out what I really wanted to do and finish my education degree. I took about ten biology and science-related classes before I realized I absolutely HATED it. I tried psychology next and took five courses, but quickly learned that while I am a helper, I didn't want to dig that deep into how people think. I took a semester off and substituted in a high school quite a lot, and I fell in love with it. Teaching kids how to think is my thing, and twelfth graders are my absolute specialty.

High school seniors are truly the best grade. They are so close to being adults, but they're still ignorant baby fools. It's a wonderful mix. By the end of the year, they're miniature adults with more reasoning skills and maturity. They're still fools, but teenager fools. We aim for growth not perfection.

I click to open the email, and my heart drops when I read the exact same rejection form they sent me twice before. I want to buy a house. I want to travel. I want an adult savings account. How the hell am I supposed to live with these student loan payments that are higher than my rent? I lay my head on my desk and breathe through my desire to sob.

Markita sings the song and sounds like a miniature Whitney herself. I smile and get out of my seat and start snapping as Markita repeats the same two lines over and over again.

"What do you know about Ms. Whitney?" I ask, turning the music down.

"Miss Turner, I know she had big hair and was famous in the 1900s." I grind my teeth and attempt to reset the conversation before they destroy my self-esteem and make me feel ancient. The 1900s. I can't stand this generation.

"All right, we are going to do silent discussions today based on your reading last night." Groans reverberate through my classroom; music to my ears, and it's the most noise they will make today. They despise silent discussions. All of their thoughts have to be written down.

"Sir Lancelot, tell me the rules of silent discussion."

"No talking, initial your writing, answer at least four questions, and add comments to five other people's answers." He lists them off on his fingers.

"Yeah, but you missed everyone's favorite one. What is it?"

"Textual evidence."

"Yep! Ok, take about five minutes to review the reading. We are discussing the different themes, so I hope you highlighted some evidence and wrote down the themes from yesterday."

My chart paper is already up and ready. The markers are out. I love setting up a class for an activity. Sometimes I wish I'd been an elementary teacher, but little kids throw up and pee themselves too much for me. And they whine, and their parents complain, and I don't actually like little kids.

Porsche comes swirling in almost immediately after my last student leaves my classroom.

"Did you leave before your kids did?" I chuckle. She loves her job, but she's done at 3:30 p.m. every day and not a minute after.

"I let them leave two minutes early. I'm tired. And my feet hurt in these shoes."

"No one told your high-maintenance ass to wear those heels to work."

"You never know whose weekend daddy ended up with them for the week. I had parking lot duty this morning. Some freshmen get dropped off still. You know I love a weekend daddy! There's nothing better than some Wednesday wings and single-daddy dick." I get up from my desk and close my classroom door. God, she's every bit of too much all the time.

"Something is wrong with you," I screech, shaking my head.

"Everything is right with me. Anyway, what's good?"

"Nothing," I groan, opening my laptop and turning the screen so she can see my rejection email. I put my head down on my desk again. Porsche's application was accepted on her first try. She even did my second application for me. It just doesn't make any sense.

"Dammit Reese. I'm sorry." She hobbles over to me in her ridiculous shoes and gives me a hug. I lean into it and tamp down the jealousy that always rises when I'm around her. She is the lucky one in our trio of friends. Everything works out for her perfectly with no fuss, and I really don't understand it. Not that she doesn't deserve the best of everything, but is she the only one who deserves it?

"You know what you need, right?"

"An OnlyFans account?" In my head, I'm deciding if I'll just do foot stuff or go full on hardcore.

"Bitch, what?!" She steps back from me, then pauses. "Actually, that can be plan B. You got the schoolgirl thing going strong. You could make a little money. But I was going to say you need a sugar daddy. It's more discreet than OnlyFans, but you might have to actually give up some ass."

"Do you just suppress who you really are all day in the classroom then unleash it on me?"

"I mean..." She shrugs. "Yeah, that's what I do. Why?"

I shake my head at her and start packing up my bag. Tomorrow, the kids are writing, so it's a low prep and low energy day for me except that I will be grading essays all day long. I keep the chart paper up so they can use what they silently discussed today in their essays tomorrow. I run a well-oiled machine that puts all the teaching at the beginning of the week and all the activities, discussions, writing and tests at the end. I'm locked into my weekly routine. It only took me eight years to get here.

Those first few years were beyond tough, and I was well on my way to becoming a statistic in the teaching profession. I don't do it for the money because where even is it? But I do love the schedule. Working from eight until 3:30 plus fall break, winter break, spring break, and summer break makes it worth it for me. I completely dissociate from my job, and I have no regrets.

Tonight, after stopping by the farmer's market to get ingredients for the dish I'm making in our weekly BFF potluck, I'm going to fill out some applications. I don't need a new job, but I do need a part-time job. These student loans are ruining my life.

Subscribe to my newsletter High on Love to stay caught up on what's going on in my writer world including upcoming novels!

Chapter 2

Dru

Madeline Martin, who refuses to even consider going by M&M even though she's the exact same color as the chocolate inside and her signature red lipstick matches the candy coating, commands our dinner table as she has since we were children. She commands it like she does the boardroom of SoftScape, the luxury bedding company she founded twenty years ago bringing our family from the middle class to the highest level of upper class.

We rented a three bedroom house for years, and I know my parents struggled at times, but Mom's ingenuity, hard work, and dedication to her company literally helped us do what most people never do, move up in class.

"Dru Landon Martin," she begins, and I perk up and put my phone down. I'd been checking the numbers on my latest post. Anything less than 10,000 is a failure in my eyes, but the last video I posted of me prepping for a business meeting in my office hit 50,000.

"I'm ready to retire. And you know as my youngest and my businessman, SoftScape is yours. Well, it should be. Hopefully it will be."

I frown. What does she mean "hopefully"? It's been common

knowledge since I graduated with my MBA that I'd take over SoftScape. What's she talking about?

"You're too focused on your job, Dru. Too focused on money and social media and work. When was the last time you brought a girl home? Not just to your bed?" My face gets hot. Mom should never bring up my sex life, and even more never at the dinner table.

"Ma!"

"I'm serious Dru. You will not take over this company and live your manicured life through your phone. I have enough pillows and comforters. I need grandchildren."

Dreya clears her throat. Mom is holding Dreya's three-week-old daughter. She rocks Jurnee, places a kiss on her forehead, and looks up at me.

"More. I need more grandchildren, Dru."

I'm thirty years old, and although my mom and dad provided us with the best life has to offer, I still acquired my own wealth. I run my own company, a company whose popularity I built with social media. One that no one has any idea I am about to sell for an astronomical price.

I'm the littlest brother of the family, the technology zombie, and the playboy, but I move in silence. I'm selling my company because I know my mom wants to hand over the reins, and I plan to be a fully invested, active CEO. I've been ready to take over for a while now.

"What are you saying?" I ask, leaning in closer to the table.

"I'm saying I will not retire until you are settled down with someone."

"Settled down? What does settled down look like?" I know she's not talking about marriage. I don't even have a girlfriend right now.

Jurnee starts to fuss, so Mom gets up and walks around the dining room rocking her. I haven't seen Mom this happy in a while. She only wants to be Glam-Ma. But I damn sure am not ready to be married.

"I think she's hungry, Mom. You can do just about everything I can for her, but you can't feed her."

"I could if you'd give her a bottle."

"Give me my baby, Mom." Dreya reaches out for Jurnee.

"I'm just kidding. Take my baby and feed her, but I want her right back." Mom's hand lingers on Jurnee's foot before she fully releases her. Then she dramatically turns to me and stares me down.

"'Settled down' means married. It means I see you head over heels, infatuated with someone. I see you in love. Do you even know what love is?" She sits back down in her chair at the head of the table. She's trying to boardroom intimidate me. She's posturing like she does when men are trying to tell her what to do.

I roll my eyes. She's on a roll, and she won't stop until she's delivered all of her daggers. I'm not going to admit to her that I have no idea what it means to be in love. I know how like feels. I also know how betrayal feels. I know about gold-digging. I know pain. I prefer success because it's attainable and hard to take away from me.

"I created this company to give our family a better life, not to make it become my life or your life, Sweetheart. It's supposed to allow us comfort and time together. And I can just see you holed up in your office all day and all night worrying over how to make even more money. I want babies. I want joy and laughter. I want family vacations with my children and their spouses. I want to enjoy everyone in my retirement. I do not want to worry about you." She looks me dead in my eyes.

She's not entirely wrong about me and SoftScape. I'm already toying with some ideas to increase sales and some new products to offer. Expanding online sales and offering personalized items are my top two directives. I can do all of that and find a wife. I don't need a wife before I take over.

"Ma, I'm going to take SoftScape to another level. Look at my own company. I did it as an experiment to see what I am capable of. You've seen the numbers."

"Do you love it, Son?" Dad finally had something to say, but he wasn't on my side either.

"Do I love it?"

"I love that it currently stands as the number one meal prep company in the country. I love the revenue it brings in." I pull out my phone to show them the numbers, but they both wave me off.

"No, Son," my dad begins. "Do you love the business aspect: the meetings, marketing, running the teams, thinking of new ideas? It sounds like you love the lifestyle and the power."

"I love being productive and making money."

My mother nods. "Exactly. So, I won't be retiring until you get married. I am weary and tired and too old to still be doing this, but I won't let you sacrifice your chance at happiness."

After dinner, I want my bed. I should have known Mom was on her bull when she requested a Wednesday night family dinner. We don't do that. She's lucky Dreya and I were free. Draymond and Drummond are lucky they are out of the country on business. Neither of them has expressed interest in taking over the company. Both of them pursued other lucrative passions after college. I'm the only one looking to keep the family legacy alive.

I'm going to blame Dreya and Jurnee—yes, I'm blaming my newborn niece. Mom has baby fever by proxy, and Dreya can't give her another one yet. The twins are the next oldest, so they should be next on the list of baby demands. They aren't married yet either, so I don't know why she's singling me out.

Dreya: This isn't my fault.

I laugh out loud at my sister's text. She has to be using telepathy right now to read my thoughts.

Me: How'd you know I was thinking it was?

Dreya: Because you always think her latest initiatives that you are sucked into are my fault. I'm not that into you, little bro.

Me: Whatever. Send me a picture of my niece so I can have a reason to smile.

Chapter 3

Charisse

I wanted to stay home tonight. On Saturday evenings, I usually binge-watch dating reality tv while eating gluten-free cookies. I had also planned to fill out more part-time job applications, but Lily had other plans for me and for Porsche. I'm the boring friend. Porsche is the wild friend, and Lily is the artsy friend. We are a well-rounded trio. Lily works a traditional job, but her side hustle and passion is doing paint and sip pop-ups. She creates an amazing atmosphere, and the pieces people create at her events are nothing short of amazing. Lily's paint and sip pop-ups have become the talk of the town. Tonight's theme is plants, and she requested the presence of her best friends.

I don't have kids, but I have plant babies. Lily used one of my Monstera Deliciosas as her model for this event. I can't not be there for my child's public debut. No one will leave with an ugly canvas. I'm going to make sure everyone creates a beautiful rendition of her.

I slide hangers to the left in my closet as I try to pick out what to wear. I move right on past all of my work outfits. I refuse to even wear one article of teacher clothes. Do I want to be sexy? Do sugar daddies go to paint and sip pop-ups? I pick a body-con tank top dress that hits midway up my thigh. It shows a little something-something without me needing to worry about bending over or crossing my leg too aggressively and showing everyone in my room my OnlyFans content. It's green. I wonder if it matches the painting too much, but I look damn good in green, and that's my goal tonight.

Looking at my shoe collection, I ask myself, "What would Porsche wear?" A pair of sparkly, golden heels jump out at me. Yeah, she would absolutely wear these. I channel Porsche to get out of teacher mode. She's been wild since we met, probably before we met, dancing to the music of her personal soundtrack. Porsche doesn't know how to be anyone but herself. Either you love her or you hate her. And I can't help but to love her.

I arrive at Porsche's door, having picked the designated driver straw for tonight. I'll just drink when I get home. I'm early because I know she's not ready yet, but she will need me to push her to finish in time.

"You're trying to snag a sugar daddy tonight!" She holds my hand above my head, and I give her a little twirl.

"If one finds me, so be it!" I'm pretty sure she's serious about this sugar daddy business, but I'm absolutely not—I think. I don't need a man to pay my bills; I need to hit the lottery. That's all. But catching a cute guy's attention tonight won't hurt. Lily's paint and sips attract all kinds of people, including single men who come on a quest for women. Who knows what the night holds?

I help zip her skin-tight minidress with a keyhole back. She does various bends, testing out which ones won't cause a scandal at the event. Short answer: all of them will, but Porsche doesn't care. She shouldn't because she looks like a goddess. Turquoise makes her shine. It's definitely her color. She piles her braids up into a tall bun and chooses earrings while I pick out a clutch for her from her vast collection.

The music thumps when we enter the atrium of Serenity

Garden. I've only passed by it because I'll go ham buying plants if I ever ended up here. I'm instantly drawn to the gorgeous greenery lining the windows, ditching Porsche to take photos of plants I will definitely come back and buy. The atmosphere is peaceful, even with Lily's music. She loves to set the tone with music; today Sade's smooth and soothing voice does the trick. I sway to the rhythm and caress a leaf or two before Lily spots me.

"I knew you'd be over here. I kept looking over here for you and not even at the door."

"They have a Birkin. I've been wanting one forever."

"The bag?" Porsche asks as she walks up to us.

"Girl, no! I don't even have a honey daddy, much less a sugar daddy. There's no way I can afford a Birkin bag. It's the plant. A Philodendron Birkin." I trace the stripes on the leaves with my hand.

"You need to quit teaching and become a botanist, weirdo."

Lily and I giggle and shake our heads at Porsche. She doesn't want anything alive in her apartment except for her. Lily, like me, has an affinity for plants. Her plant love extends to growing her own (along with mine and Porsche's) produce in her backyard garden.

"We are starting in about five minutes, so figure out where you're sitting and get yourselves refreshments." She walks off, greeting people as she makes her way to her station.

The tables are set up in a giant U shape with Lily's table in the center where everyone can see. The music gets softer, and Lily announces that we will be starting soon.

"Where do you want to sit?" Neither of us take the seats at the

13

center of the U. We leave those for paying customers. Porsche directs us to sit next to two very handsome men, and I don't have any complaints.

"Hello." One of the men leans over. "I'm Marcus, and this is my homie Dru. I couldn't not introduce myself to you two absolutely beautiful women." Dru looks up at us and offers a smile.

"Well, hello Marcus. Why don't you come over here and sit by me?" Porsche pats the seat I am about to sit in. I step back and let Marcus have it, and I take up my spot next to Dru. I'm not shocked that Porsche immediately put me out. Marcus is very sexy. He's just her type: dark brown skin, a sexy, hypnotic smile, and charisma oozing from him. I know for sure that Porsche isn't the only woman in this place eyeing him. She's the only one confident enough to tell him to sit by her though. And he listened like the love-sick puppy he's about to be.

I channel Porsche and attempt to strike up a conversation with Dru.

"Hi Dru," I offer, peeking over at him. He's not unattractive. He's actually even cuter than Marcus. His skin has more of a red tone to it. His eyes are dark, almost black. I can lose my soul if I stare into them for too long. He's built too, with massive shoulders. His sleeves are fighting for their lives with his arms filling them out.

Before he gets a chance to answer, Lily speaks on the microphone excitedly telling us about what we will be painting. She stands at the front of her table, her arms crossed and that sweet Lily smile on her face.

"Welcome, everyone!" she says cheerfully. "I'm Lily, your instructor for the evening. I'm so excited to see all of you here at Lit with Lily tonight."

The group chatters excitedly, some of us sipping on glasses of wine, while others fidget with their paint brushes and canvases.

"So, are you all ready to get started?" Lily asks, gesturing to the tables lined with paints and brushes. "Let's begin by picking out our colors."

She walks over to a table filled with a rainbow of paint tubes and holds one up.

"This is cadmium red," she says. "It's a great color for adding pops of warmth to your painting."

Lily goes on to explain the other colors, giving tips and tricks for creating different hues and shades.

"Now, let's talk about brushes," she continues. "You'll want to use a larger brush for the background and a smaller brush for the details. And don't forget to rinse your brush between colors."

She's so engaging. Even talking about paint and paint brushes captures everyone's attention. People are nodding eagerly and full of smiles. I never really paid attention before, but this must be so much fun to do. It's teaching people who actually want to learn—teaching people who PAY you to learn.

"Okay, now it's time to start painting!" Lily exclaims. "Remember, there are no mistakes in art, only happy accidents. So don't worry if it doesn't look perfect at first. Just have fun and let your creativity flow."

I look over at Porsche, and she's more focused on Marcus than on painting. I look at Dru, and he's hyper focused on painting. I guess I'm on my own.

I watch Lily begin the painting, starting with the flower pot.

My lines almost match hers, so I am content to begin filling the outline in with paint. Beside me, Dru grumbles. Trying my best to keep my eyes on my own canvas, I work on the stems coming out of the vase.

"The hell?" Dru stopped painting; he's pouting.

"Do you need some help?" The teacher in me cannot sit around while someone gives up.

"My lines are jagged. I'm not sure how it can be helped." I stand up and take a look at his whole canvas, and I burst out laughing. Shame on teacher me, but he's drawn an upside down step pyramid.

"You're just gonna dog me out..."

"Charisse."

"Charisse. I'm not sure I want your help if it includes you laughing at my work." I take a deep breath.

"I'm sorry. You're right. I wasn't expecting steps though. It's an inverted ziggurat. I shouldn't have laughed. I'm awful."

"I told you it wasn't fixable though."

"Everything is fixable...except student loans."

He turns to face and raises his eyebrows.

"Nevermind. You can just make your pot bigger. Monstera don't really like bigger pots because they want their roots to be close together, but this is a painting." He continues to stare at me. I breathe in slowly through my nose. This man makes me nervous and chatty and maybe a little hot and bothered.

"Here, trace the corners of all of your steps here in a diagonal

16

line." I take his brush from him and start the line.

"Then you'll just fill the whole thing in with paint. You can even put decorative accents on the outside of the pot when the base color dries."

"Thank you, Charisse." Hearing my name come out of his mouth gives me the tiniest shiver up my spine.

"Charisse, how's it going over there?" Lily stops giving instructions and moves about the room, checking in on people.

"It's going well." She places her hand on my shoulder.

"And how about you?" She's looking at Dru's canvas, and he's just about finished fixing his stair-step flower pot.

"Your helpful assistant, Charisse, has me on track." He looks over at me and smiles then he takes out his phone and takes a picture of his canvas.

"Well, she's an actual teacher, so it makes sense that she would be helping someone do better. She's a good one." She winks at me and keeps walking.

"What do you teach?" His eyes are going back and forth between Lily's unfinished painting and to his as he works to paint the stems in the flower pot exactly like Lily's

"High school English—seniors to be exact."

"Ooh, is that high-pressure?"

I scrunch my face. I've never been asked that.

"No, I wouldn't say it is. Why do you ask?"

"You have to get them ready for the real world. That's a lot of responsibility. I don't know much about teaching, but I do know that English teachers do a lot. I remember that from high school."

"You aren't wrong about that. I guess I just don't see it as stressful. It's just what I do."

"What about you? What do you do?"

"I work in business." He offers me nothing else, and I don't pry. I look at Porsche; she's grown bored with Marcus.

"How's it going over there, Porsche?" I lean back.

"It's all right." She turns to Marcus. "Can you move back to your first seat? I want to sit with my girl now." I close my eyes and stifle my laugh. She's ridiculous. He obliges, and we both fumble with our canvases and paints to get switched back to how we were when we began.

"You are too much!" I laugh at her and at the fact that Marcus just accommodated her without a sound.

"He's married."

My eyes bug out at her.

"He's what? He moved seats and sat by you, and the whole time he was married?"

"To his job. He's married to his job, girl. He stayed on his phone the whole time and barely engaged with me. Look, he didn't paint that much. Why did he come?"

My relief comes out in a giggle that I cannot contain. I sit there and laugh for a solid thirty seconds before I get it together enough to follow Lily's directions.

The event ends with us milling around the refreshments table and Porsche downing a few more glasses of wine. Dru and Marcus left right when we all finished the paintings, not even giving their creations a chance to dry. I did get to see how tall Dru is. He is tall enough to climb. He's got to be a ladies' man. He's too fine to be single.

Chapter 4

Dru

I should have asked for her number. I barely got her name. What can I do with just her first name? Marcus completely fumbled it with her friend. She's the exact type of girl he needs. He is addicted to his phone though—married to his job like my mom doesn't want me to be. I have to at least start dating. I need this company, so I need a wife.

I sit in my office, looking out the window at the SoftScape retail store. I check in to see what's selling well and what's not ever so often, and I haven't been lately. I should be heading out of the office soon anyway, so I'll stop in.

"Charisse?" She is heading toward the door as I walk in. She looks up a little too late and nearly bumps into me.

"Oh, hey! Dru, right?"

"Yeah. Are you looking for some sheets or pillows?"

"No, I'm looking for a job. I have to get my student loans paid off. I'm tired of being teacher poor...not that I needed to tell all my business to you."

I laugh. "No, I understand. Who did you interview with?"

"Um." She pulls out her phone. "Greta. She's the person who called me today to set it up. It was pure luck that she called during my lunch period, or I would have missed it. I think it went pretty well. How about you?"

An idea comes to mind, and I don't know if I should go for it, but I decide to leap before I look.

"You may not know this, but my mother is actually the founder of this company."

"I did not know that." She tries to hide her shock.

"Yeah. Come over here with me." I walk her over to some chairs they have set up toward the back of the showroom. We sit, and I continue.

"So, this is going to sound crazy. It actually is crazy, but hear me out all the way, ok?"

Her face is blank. If she's thinking anything at all, she's hiding it so well.

"Last week, my mother told me that I had to get married to be able to take over the company. She is ready to retire since my sister had a baby, and she wants to be a Glam-Ma." I chuckle because that word is so goofy to say out loud.

"Ok?" Confusion is setting in.

"Stay with me." My heart rate has to have doubled. I can feel it in my ears. "Since you need to make some extra money to pay off your student loans, and I need a wife to take over SoftScape, what do you think about us having an arrangement where we can both attain our goals?"

"Dru, what the hell are you talking about?" Her confusion has morphed into annoyance. She is sitting up straighter and has her arms crossed over her chest.

"I'm asking you to marry me?" It sounds just as terrible as it should. Poor girl. I bet she has a dream proposal thought up in her head, and here I am—basically a stranger— proposing a fake marriage to her in the back of SoftScape.

Silence follows my proposal. That's the right response, I think. I'd do the same thing if the roles were reversed. I let her simmer on my question for a good minute, thinking out some of the details.

"It will be a legal agreement. We can draw up terms. I will pay you in increments."

"How much?" I can see her wheels turning.

"I really don't know. It would have to be at least a year long commitment. Does a million seem fair?"

She squeaks like a mouse and slumps back in the chair.

"Are you all right? 1.5 million? Is that better?" Dedicating a year to faking a marriage is worth that much, I think.

"Can I have some time to think about it?"

"Sure, sure you can. You won't need this job if you agree. I'll have my attorney draw something up right now, and I can email it to you. Can you give me your info?" I open the notes app on my phone and hand it to her. Her hands are shaky as she takes it from me.

I call Hunter Mitchell, one of my college buddies and my

personal lawyer. I think Charisse might go for this. I could see her thoughts swirling as we parted.

"Hey, Hunt! Are you busy?"

"Not really. I'm waiting for my food to be delivered. Other than that, I'm chilling with Cozy." Hunter is the only man I know who can pull off having a chihuahua as a pet. That dog is his child. No one understands it. We all just let him live though.

"I have a top-secret request. It needs to be more confidential than anything has ever been."

"Did you get someone pregnant?"

"No! I might be getting married."

"Word? I didn't know you were dating anyone. That's great! So you need me to write up a prenup?"

"Not exactly. I need a marriage contract. I'm paying her $1.5 million to marry me and stay with me for a year. I need you to hammer out all the details including that we have to live together. Consummating the marriage is not required. I can't even think of everything that needs to be in there, but I trust that you can. I need it pretty quickly, within the next two hours."

More silence. Rendering people speechless is today's special skill.

"Are you still there?" He's been quiet for a whole minute now.

"Yeah, I—uh..."

"So confidentiality will be important, but so is being able to confide in your people, so have an NDA ready for any friends she may have that she wants to talk to about this. I'm going to see if she'll meet me for dinner tonight to discuss it. Can you get it taken care of?"

"Yes, I can."

"Great, send it to me when you're finished."

Once I pull into my spot in the parking garage, I open my notes app and call Charisse.

"Hello, Dru?" Her voice is breathy, almost a whisper.

"Hi, I'm sorry to bother you, but I wanted to see if you'd join me for dinner tonight. We can talk more about this potential arrangement and see what we are both comfortable with. I can get the private room at The Sapphire at 6:30. Is that okay with you?"

Maybe after we are married, I'll let her know that I own the restaurant.

"Sure, that would be nice. I do have some questions."

I smile. This just might work.

"Ok, text me your address. I'll be there at 6."

I send out a few texts as I take the elevator up to my suite. The Sapphire is set, and my driver will be here in thirty-five minutes. I hurry into my place to get ready. I should have my own questions, but nothing comes to mind. I'm just excited that I may have outsmarted my mother. That remains to be seen.

Chance parks outside Charisse's apartment. I'm happy he's driving because apartment complexes have always confused me. They never seem to be in numerical order. Chance found her apartment building and number instantly. He knows this town inside and out.

"It's on the ground floor, Sir."

"Thank you." I step out of the SUV and straighten my suit. For a moment, I pause and worry that I did not tell her the dress requirements for the restaurant. It was presumptuous of me to think everyone automatically knows.

I knock on her door and hold my breath when I hear it unlock. This is the craziest thing I've ever tried to do.

The first thing I notice when she opens the door is her smile. It is bright and genuine, not forced or uncomfortable. She might actually be happy to see me.

"Hi! Please come in. I just need to put on my jewelry. I had to google The Sapphire to see what I should wear. I hope this is nice enough." She stands up in front of me and does a dainty turn. She's wearing coral, which looks amazing against her honey brown skin. It makes her glow. The top is going to drive me wild. When I had to go wedding dress shopping with my sister, I learned all the dress lingo, and I know for sure that this dress has a sweetheart neckline that is barely containing her cleavage. When she turns, I notice her ass for the first time since I met her, which is surprising because I notice ass first and foremost all the time. She must know how to downplay it for work. I left the paint and sip in a rush, and I don't even think I ever saw her get up.

"Your dress is perfect." I clear my throat. I want to say so much more, but I have to calm down. I can't be attracted to my fake wife. That would mess everything up. We need to set that rule immediately.

"You look beautiful."

She smiles at me before rushing to the back of her apartment.

"Is it cold in there? Will I need a shawl?"

"I'm never cold there, but I'm usually wearing something like this. I don't think it would hurt to bring it. My sister brings a shawl or jacket or even a blanket with her everywhere."

She comes out of the back wearing diamond stud earrings and a necklace. They complete the look.

"Ok, I'm ready to go." She's shoving things into a clutch. "Ok, maybe not. Where are my keys?" She rushes back into the bedroom. I look around me and see them hanging on a hook by her door.

"Charisse? They're hanging up out here." I jingle them.

"Oh my gosh! I never use that! It doesn't matter, does it? I lose them if I don't use it, and I lose them if I do?" She laughs at herself as I open the door for her.

Chance is there to open the car door for us. She looks back at me as she climbs in.

"A driver, huh? This alone might sway me."

I chuckle. This is one of my favorite luxuries.

"There's so much more than this." I climb in next to her.

"Do tell." She crosses her legs and turns her body toward me.

"Well, I already told you my mother is the founder and CEO of SoftScape. I founded my own company right after college, and it has taken off. Don't tell anyone, but I'm actually in talks to sell it. I should be closing the deal in the next week or two."

"Wow! I often wonder what my life would have been like had I been born into wealth or even just the middle class. I clawed my way out of poverty just to have the cost of my education threaten to put me right back down." Sadness briefly sweeps across her face.

"Can I ask what company you started? And why is your mother's company so important to you if you have your own?"

"My company is Fresh Flavor Fix."

Her eyes get big.

"You know it?"

"I do! I cheat sometimes with my weekly potlucks with my girls and use some of Triple F's meals instead of going to the store or the farmer's market to get fresh ingredients. They can never tell the difference, and there's enough choices to fit all of our weird themes."

"That's great feedback! To answer your second question, I'm the youngest, probably the most spoiled, and I want to prove my worth by taking over. None of my siblings want anything to do with the company, but I want to help keep it alive and move it into the future. Have you seen our website? It's pathetic, and the warehouses need a serious upgrade. Mom is all about the in-store experience, but she doesn't understand that most people buy online. It's my family's legacy."

She nods, taking in everything I've said.

When we get to the restaurant, Chance parks right outside the entrance and opens the car door for me. I step out and take Charisse's hand. All eyes are on us as we make our way to the private room. Actually, all eyes are on Charisse. She's built for this kind of life, and the reaction to her from the patrons of my restaurant tells me just that.

My phone dings, and it is the contract coming in from Hunter. I clear my throat. We just got settled, and I don't know if we need to immediately jump into business.

"Do you want to order first, or do you want to get down to business?" I'm anxious to check out this contract, even though I know Hunter has done it right. Nervous doesn't even begin to describe how I feel about this whole situation. It's outrageous, but it can also be the key to everything.

"I want to order. I can't think on an empty stomach, and I am starving." She rubs her stomach.

I wave the waiter over and ask her to bring a couple of the best appetizers to our table. She slips away quietly and returns almost instantly with the Mezze Platter and a big plate of spanakopita.

"These look delicious!" Charisse put her menu down and eyes the platters in front of us.

"Are you ready to order?" I look to Charisse, allowing her to order first.

"Yes, I'll have the sea bass." She picks up a pita chip and dips it in the hummus. I can't tell if she's being dainty for show or if that's just who she is. The chip has the slightest dab of hummus on it. Will she even be able to taste it?

"The sea bass is my favorite here. I'll have the same." We sit in silence. I want to take out my phone and look over the contract first, but that would be rude. She's really enjoying the food, and it's kind of nice watching her. She has gorgeous lips and flawless skin. My mom is going to adore her.

Chapter 5

Charisse

This food is otherworldly. I know it's expensive, so I'm going to eat everything put in front of me. I'm trying to not feel a way about the fact that he ordered the same thing as me because I won't be able to taste his food.

I'm not getting serial killer vibes from him. And I can absolutely get used to this lifestyle for the year he wants me to be married to him. As long as this contract has no sex involved, I'm going to say yes. I've already decided.

Dru is anxious. Sweat beads at his temples. I pause my eating to really take him in. He's unbelievably handsome. And before I can form the whole thought, I ask him why he's single.

"I, uh—well."

I laugh way louder than necessary in this private room. The kitchen and dining room had to have heard it. I cover my mouth.

"I'm sorry. That's not my business, and that was rude. It's just that you're really good looking and obviously very wealthy. You don't seem like an ass, so I can't put two and two together, unless you drown yourself in work and don't have time for anything else." His eyes grow big, and I have my answer.

"Ah, got it. So if I say yes to this, what exactly is expected of me?"

"I'm glad you asked." His smile is so sexy, and his lips look so soft.

"My lawyer emailed me this contract a few minutes ago." He moves his chair next to mine and holds his phone up for us to both read.

"I haven't looked it over yet. And it is tentative. Anything we decide to change can be added."

The biggest rules in the contract say that we have to get engaged publicly, live together after the engagement, stay married for seventeen months, and there's no consummation required.

"I thought you said 1.5million," I whisper, trying to keep my breathing steady after reading that I'd get 2.5 million.

"Hunter extended the time and added more tasks. The added publicity and time made him feel the number should be higher, and I don't disagree. He was smart to put seventeen months on there. Breaking up at exactly one year would be highly suspicious. Mom would be on that so fast. So would the rest of my family. I already have to get the idea that I've been dating you out in the atmosphere. I mean, if we are doing this."

I'd consummate the marriage for this amount. I'm not telling him that.

"We are doing this. Where do I sign?"

He sits back in his chair, surprise all over his face.

"Do we need to make any additions to the contract?"

I furrow my brows, trying to think of anything that needs to change. Nothing comes to mind. "Not that I can think of, but can we add something that says we can amend this if something we hadn't thought of comes up, but in lawyer speak?"

He nods and sends a text.

"I'll have Hunter add that and send us a new one right now. It'll be in your email in a few minutes. "

"Oh, I need to tell my girls. Can they just sign an NDA?"

"Yes, absolutely. Is two people enough?"

I consider his question. For this to work, my family needs to believe it too. If I can tell Lily and Porsche, I should be able to survive the next almost two years.

"Yes. It'll just be my two best friends. You met them both at the paint and sip." He's texting, but he nods to acknowledge me.

"Ok, Hunter needs their email addresses. He won't send them until you let him know that you've spoken to them. But getting all the paperwork taken care of at once will help him out a lot." He hands me his phone, and I type in the girls' full names and email addresses.

"I can't believe I'm doing this."

He chuckles. "I can't believe it either. I did not think you would say yes."

"Really? Who would say no to fake marrying a handsome, wealthy man for $2.5 million? Oh! I just got the contract." I quickly open my email and sign it.

"Done!" I'm actually excited. Nothing good or exciting ever really happens to me. This is going to be an adventure.

He walks me to my door at the end of the night. This almost felt like a date—one of my better dates. Maybe the best date in a while.

"Expect a timeline of events by the end of the week. Something you should know about me is that I am a meticulous planner."

I nod at him and smile, thinking maybe I will learn some great things from this super successful man.

"Thank you for a wonderful evening."

"Thank you for accepting my bootleg proposal. I promise the next one will be amazing." He reaches out and touches my arm and smiles.

"I'll be sure to be amazed."

Behind my closed door, I cheese from ear to ear. I get to live the best lie there is for close to two years and make...my stomach tightens at the thought of the number. It is unbelievable. A text comes through from Dru with Hunter's number, so I can let him know when to send the contracts to Porsche and Lily . After I put my to-go boxes in the fridge, I video call Lily and Porsche.

"Shouldn't you be asleep? It's 9 p.m." Porsche always has jokes about my early bedtime. A good sleep schedule means a good life.

"I have some news, but hold on." I text Hunter to let him know to email the NDA's in about five minutes.

"Are you all absolutely alone?" I can't blow this in the first hour.

"Now you know I don't have a man. I'm as alone as you are. Why you asking rude ass questions?"

"Oh my gosh, Porsche. Are you alone in your home right now? I have something confidential to tell you. Geez!"

"I'm alone." I love Lily. She's just a bottle of peace.

"Yeah, I'm alone. What do you have?"

I want to give them a dramatic story, but I didn't rehearse anything.

"I'm getting married!" I blurt out.

"Congratulations!" Lily offers, forever not pressing an issue and happy for me no matter what.

"Congratulations? Really Lily? We don't know who. She isn't dating anyone, and you know that. What the hell are you talking about, Charisse?" She is peering into the phone now, and all I can see is her eyeball.

"So, remember that handsome guy I sat next to at the paint and sip?"

"The one with the sexy but boring friend? Yeah. You just met him a few days ago. You can't be engaged to him."

"Yes, I can be, and I am. I was at SoftScape for a job interview, and he was there because his mom started the company. She wants to retire, but she won't give it to him until he settles down."

"Ooookay." Porsche is rarely speechless, but this seems like it's about as close to that as we are going to get.

"So, he proposed to me at SoftScape." Both of them stare at me with open mouths. I sit in the silence waiting to hit them with the good stuff.

"Ok, so you met him on Saturday, saw him today—Monday, and now you're engaged." Lily is speaking slowly and carefully.

Trying to be supportive but also questioning my common sense and decision-making. Porsche's face tells me she's really trying to figure it out. I think she might get it, so I drag the silence out.

"Bitch, is he paying you?"

I crack up.

"Yes! Yes! Yes! $2.5 million! So go ahead and sign the NDA in your email because I am under an actual, legal contract."

"Wait, wait, wait!" Lily's eyes are squinting at me through the phone. "Who is this guy? How do you know he has the money?"

Damn, I never even thought about it. I just took him at face value. I can't let them know that. This is already ridiculous. I secretly pray that he's legit.

"Dru Martin. His mom is Madeline Martin. He also started Fresh Flavor Fix."

"Ok, so all of that checks out, so far." Porsche has her laptop open.

"Let me see his net worth." She clicks a few keys on her keyboard.

"Holy shit! He's got the money. What he's paying you is actually a drop in the bucket for him. He is an actual billionaire. A one percenter. I told you to get a sugar daddy, and you upped the ante. You're marrying a billionaire. A fine ass billionaire. Please tell me sex is in the contract? Please, please, please!"

"I recall the contract specifically saying no consummation is required. And I am a means to an end. So is he. No feelings. No love. We may have to do some public kissing and canoodling, but there will be no sex."

"Why not? Sweeten the deal," Porsche adds.

Lily interjects, "So, we are the only two people in your life who know about this? Who will know about this? You're going to lie to your parents? To your sister? And have them believe you've met Mr. Right, a billionaire, and believe this marriage is legit?"

I haven't thought about any of that in detail. I saw the money. I guess this is the "what could go wrong?" part.

"It's a small sacrifice for the financial security it will give me"

Lily's face is serious, and she's shaking her head. "They're going to be so excited and so happy for you. They'll fly out and spend money on all the extravagance of the wedding and have this beautiful idea of the two of you in their heads, and then in seventeen months, poof, it's gone?"

"He's going to pay for everything about the wedding," Porsche butts in, clearly down for this ruse until the wheels fall off. This is who my girls are. Porsche is the ride or die. Lily is conscientious. They are my balance. There's nothing to say in response to Lily. The contract is signed. I didn't even have a lawyer look at it for me to make sure I'm protected. I just saw the payout.

"I understand your trepidation, Lily. I need you and Porsche to support me through this though. And I need you both to sign the NDA right now. I'm mentally exhausted, and I need to get to bed. I still have to be a poor teacher tomorrow morning. Love you guys!"

I quickly end the video call before either of them has anything to say. I start undressing and getting ready to shower when my phone dings with a text message.

Dru: Thank you for joining me for dinner tonight and for saying yes. Hunter said he got the NDA's, so we are a go.

Me: Yes, it was a bit of a hard sell with one of my friends, but we will work it out.

Dru: I get that. Hunter will be my only confidant. I don't trust anyone else to not spill the beans.

Me: I understand that.

Dru: Are you nervous?

Me: Yes, but I'm also excited. My friends googled you.

Dru: Oh man. What does that mean?

Me: It means I get to have the time of my life for the next 17 months.

There's no response for a while.

Dru: My bad. I was laughing. So you did the net worth search?

I smile. He's got a sense of humor about it.

Me: My friend Porsche did.

Dru: She's a good friend. So, then you pick the honeymoon. We are going on a nice long honeymoon wherever you want to go.

The phone falls out of my hands. Anywhere? I can't even think of anywhere to go, but knowing that money is no object makes the possibilities endless.

Dru: I'm going to email you the timeline soon. I'm still tweaking it. We need to start dating. Can we do regular Friday

night dates?

Me: Yes. I do potlucks with my friends on Saturdays and dinner out on Wednesdays. Fridays, sadly, are always open.

In the shower, my mind is swirling. I'm fake marrying a billionaire—a seemingly nice, down to earth, handsome man with money dripping off him. Can I even fake being a part of his world? I'm seriously just a poor teacher. What is life like for the wife of a billionaire?

Chapter 6

Charisse

My classroom is filled with roses when I walk in on Wednesday. Vase after vase of roses in every color under the sun. Every surface except for the students' desks has roses on it. It's overwhelming and definitely excessive. I smile through the anxiety it brings me, especially when Dr. Ranly makes his way to my room to see what the fuss is all about. The ladies in the front office helped bring them in. I'm sure the whole faculty knows at this point, and most of us have only been on campus for five minutes.

"What the fu—dge!" Porsche autocorrects herself when she spots Dr. Ranly standing' next to me upon entering my classroom.

"This is quite a spread. You've surely impressed some young man, Miss Turner. I've done this only once in my past, and that woman's name is now Mrs. Ranly." He raises his eyebrows and gives my elbow a squeeze.

"You ladies have a great day."

Porsche gives him her fakest, jovial-employee smile, which immediately drops the moment he is out the door.

"Are these from him?" She's whispering, and it's weird and

unnecessary.

"You can talk regularly. We are dating. He is my current boyfriend. You can talk about him. And yes, I don't know anyone else who could even pull this off." What time had they started bringing all of this in? I'm going to have to donate all these vases to whoever is doing prom this year.

"This is so extra. Like Tamar Braxton extra. Almost too much." Porsche walks around the room, touching the flowers.

I nod. It is. I want to be annoyed, but I have to be grateful and overjoyed.

"What the hell am I supposed to do with these in three days when they're all raggedy and disgusting? They're going to trigger someone's allergies too. And none of them are going to be able to focus with all these roses."

"Have first period deliver a vase to every teacher in the school. At least all the women. That'll get them off of your hands and maybe put a smile on everyone's face."

"Since when do you care about that? Even though that's brilliant. Crowd-sourcing in reverse!"

"I don't care. Girl, I would keep all of these flowers in here until they died and ask for more on a regular basis. They'd be all over my social media, and no one could tell me anything. But you and I are different. You should shout him out on socials though." She lowers her voice. "It'll help with visibility. Y'all do need that." I nod. She's right. I open the video app on my phone and do a little 360 around my room with a giant smile on my face.

"Thank you so much! I love them!" I end the video with a kissy face. I'll upload it after school: no posting on socials during work hours. Apparently, that's a state law now.

"So, this is the life of the rich and famous?" I sit at my desk and scoot a vase out from in front of my laptop screen.

"This is just the beginning. I'm so excited for you. I deserve an NDA trip when all is said and done. I have so many questions."

"Hmm, let me see if he can get me a private room somewhere for dinner, so we can talk freely in there. Did I tell you about The Sapphire last night?"

"The Sapphire? With the two month waiting list. I cannot."

"That Sapphire. And we were in the private room. It was so good. I have leftovers for lunch. I got fish, and I am going to stink up the whole lounge with it."

"My best friend is all grown up, living the high life with her rich ass boyfriend. I'm so proud of you!" She wipes away an imaginary tear.

"Shut up!"

"Oh, I have to send a picture to Lily!" She snaps the picture and heads back to her classroom to start her day. I sigh and look around the room. First period's lesson is a complete bust. They will be doing community service and handing out roses to every single teacher in the school. I think I'll let them record it on their phones. We will put together a montage or something. I don't know what we will do with it though. We can just keep it in the drafts.

"What the hello?" Malone screeches as she walks in. "Miss Turner, you got a boyfriend?"

I'm not ready to open this discussion up all the way.

"Someone is courting me," I tell her, smiling as I wait for a reaction. She stops in her tracks and mouths the word courting.

"Siri, what does it mean to be courting someone?"

"The definition of courting is the process of trying to attract and woo a romantic partner to create a long-term relationship or to marry the partner."

"This man is really trying to create a long-term relationship with you."

"Miss Turner, is your new man rich?"

"This is a lot of flowers. Did somebody die?"

The comments keep coming: one for each student who enters my classroom. I'm already tired.

Once the bell rings, I address the roses in the room.

"So, I met someone new. He thought a million roses was the way to impress me. It is impressive, but it's also waaaayy too much, so I have an assignment for each of you. Pick someone on campus to take a vase of roses to, record it with your phone, and email it to me. You all have seventeen minutes. Go."

They shuffle out the room full of chatter, and after the last student leaves, I realize I didn't take roll.

***

While I'm sitting in the parking lot after school, I post the video I took of the roses and tag Dru in it.

Me: Check your social media. We are official.

He calls me instead of texting me back.

"Ah, you beat me to it, but yes! That's exactly what we need. Somehow it'll get to my family. My brother uses it the most, but he will surely send it to my sister, and she will show it to Mom because Mom can barely send a text message. Family telephone." I nod my head. Family telephone is a hell of a way to communicate.

"I hate the way I'll tell my sister something I'm excited about, then I'm ready to tell my mom, but my sister beat me to it. It kills the buzz. But in this case, I think we will be just fine."

"For sure. Is now a good time to talk to you? We need to get to know each other, so I want to schedule daily talks. I'll have an agenda each day—"

A cackle escapes. There was no way to hold it back. An agenda for our daily talks? That's so robotic.

"Are you laughing at me?"

Tears are streaming down my face at this point, and I'm sucking in air. I try to take a deep breath and calm down.

"Look, I want us to be believable. We need to cover topics two people who are getting married would know about each other."

"We can get to know each other. How would you get to know a new woman you are dating?" A beat goes by.

"I would spend time with her."

Our arrangement is not that complicated. It's as easy as us getting to know each other.

"Let's start with that. Do you want to double our date nights? Do you do something regularly that I could join in?"

He's quiet, and I know that's what he does when his wheels are turning. I talk through my thinking, but he puts himself on silent mode until he's got it figured out.

"I dabble in woodwork. You can come to my workshop, and we could make some stuff together."

I pull the phone away from my ear and look at it.

"You 'dabble' in woodwork? What does that even mean? Are you a carpenter like Jesus? Are you Billionaire Black Jesus?"

The laugh that erupts on the other side of the phone is so pure and genuine. It makes me shiver.

"I am not Billionaire Black Jesus. I make things with my own two hands."

I smile at the thought of him in a shop, not in that sexy, expensive suit I saw him in when he proposed to me in the back of SoftScape. What does one do carpentry in?

"I would love to join you once a week to learn carpentry. When? Where? And what's the dress code?"

"Thursdays, 4 p.m. And I'll send a car to pick you up."

Sexier words have never been spoken to me. I can really get into having a car sent for me.

"It's a date. I've got to get going to my dinner with the girls. Oh, I meant to ask, and say no if it's not possible, but they wanted to try The Sapphire. It seems like you have an in, could you get us in tonight? I'm sure it's booked, but I wanted to ask."

There's a short pause before he answers.

"The private room is yours whenever you want it. Do you want me to send a car to pick you all up?"

I hold in my instinct to squeal.

"That would be amazing! Can the car be at my place at five?" I'm already texting the girls letting them know we've got The Sapphire's private room and a driver. We will be drinking our asses off tonight.

"It can be there whenever you want it to."

"Five is perfect. The girls all live pretty close to me, so the round up won't take too long."

***

Chance knocks on my door at exactly 5 p.m. He greets me with a big, warm smile.

"Are you ready to go, Miss Turner?"

With a quick nod and a smile in return, I grab my keys and lock up my apartment. I text Porsche to let her know we're on the way. Seven minutes later, Chance pulls into her driveway. He greets her at the door and walks her to the car. She's dressed like a disco ball: shimmery sequins adorn her jumpsuit. Her legs glisten just as brightly, although I know that's either shea butter or coconut oil.

"Hey hottie!"

"Hey Richie Rita!"

"Stop it!" I don't know if Chance knows the truth or not, and no joke is going to mess up my bag.

"Oh my bad!" She looks up at the front seat. Chance hasn't made it in the car yet.

"I can't believe this is your life right now." Porsche gestures around the SUV we are riding in.

"Me neither. Dru is spoiling me for sure. He's really sweet."

"So, are we really getting the private room at The Sapphire? I'm going to spend my whole month's grocery budget, but it'll be worth it."

"I forgot to factor in how expensive that place is." I take out my phone to check my account balance. It's good for now, but I may end up eating noodles and sandwiches for the rest of the week.

Lily is waiting on her porch for us. She's wearing a jumpsuit too, but hers has pants as opposed to Porsche's shorts, and the only sparkle is from her belt. Me and my girls are so cute.

"I like this driver business," Lily tells me as she steps into the car, holding on to Chance's hand.

"You look good, friend!" Porsche squeals.

"Thank you! I decided to try for some sophistication since we are going somewhere fancier than usual."

I snort. We usually go to Chili's. Anything is fancier than that.

We are immediately escorted to the private room. We don't even have to tell the hostess who we are.

"This is very VIP," Porsche whispers in my ear as we arrive at our table. It is much prettier than it was when I went with Dru. I send him a text letting him know I appreciate the extra care he put into our experience today.

"Miss Turner, I am told that your experience here is already paid for. Mr. Martin wanted me to make it clear that you ladies are to truly indulge and enjoy yourselves tonight. The bar is open for you, and you may order as much as you want off the menu."

"Bet!" Porsche exclaims, clapping her hands together before picking up the drink menu. "I'm going to start with a frozen strawberry margarita. I'll keep the liquor clear for tonight."

Lily and I turn to her with wide eyes and open mouths.

"What? The man said that *your* man said we could go ham. If he's going to stay your man, he needs to know who your friends are. And I, this friend right here, am greedy AF."

"You're right. It might offend him if we don't enjoy ourselves." I pick up the drink menu and ignore the prices.

"You're really sweet on him, for real. You care about his feelings. Oooh, this is so cute!" Lily claps her hands in a quick succession. I roll my eyes at her. She's just as dramatic as Porsche; it's just a different brand.

We are chatting and enjoying our hummus appetizer when I get an email from Dru.

"He just emailed me the timeline." I open the document, and I cannot contain the laughter.

"Timeline? Is he a historian?" Porsche asks, leaning into her margarita and taking a long drink from the straw.

"No," I close my eyes and huff. "He made a timeline of events to keep us on track and on the same page."

"That's nerdy but thoughtful and organized." Lily points her carrot at me as she speaks.

"So, he plans to kiss me two times on our date on Friday. There are five kisses planned on the night we get engaged. Two on the cheek, three on the lips and one to two of those will include tongue."

"Whoa, whoa, whoa! Kisses are on the timeline? This does not sound fun at all." Porsche frowns. The waiter interrupts us to take our orders. We each get something different, so we can taste each other's meals.

"It sounds respectful. You've got a respectful man. He kind of sounds like the perfect man for you. I think you're going to fall for him." Lily sips her Mai Tai and grins at me.

"I will absolutely not. He can be as perfect as he wants. But he has a goal, and so do I. That's my focus."

"Lies on lies on lies," Porsche sings out.

Neither of them knows what they're talking about. This marriage is a business arrangement, a financial transaction. Falling in love is not a part of that.

Chapter 7

Dru

It's been a hell of a day. My company acquisition is up in the air. The major brand trying to buy my company is making a big deal over minor details. I'm a details man, so for me to complain about it means they're being really nitpicky. I just want to get the sale done so I can focus on what I'm doing with Charisse. We have to do it right.

She didn't give me any feedback on the timeline. I'm not worried about it. We can discuss it tonight. I'm ready to unwind a bit and spend time with her. I've been looking forward to today. Learning more about her has been on my mind. I'm so curious about her.

She's wearing a very sexy dress today. It's skintight, showing off her absolutely perfect body. Her waist is almost impossibly small while her hips are round, grippable. I shake my head as I watch her walk in front of me to the car. I don't need to be thinking about that. We need to be planning.

"You look amazing!"

She smiles shyly. "Thank you."

We sit quietly for about a mile before she asks me a question.

"So where are we going?"

"My bad. I forgot to tell you, and it's not on the timeline. I'll add the weekly date locations." I take out my phone to remind myself.

"No, no! It's okay. I was just wondering. I like surprises and some spontaneity. It'll help make some things more believable. I think maybe you should change the engagement. I want to be able to feel something genuine."

"I understand that." I'm typing notes on my phone.

"I know you need a plan. I have surely learned that."

I smile. That is very true. If it's planned, it can be perfected. No surprises. No disappointments.

"Is that a good thing or bad thing?" I ask. Her face straightens out.

"It's neither one, I guess. Spontaneity is good; so is planning. I mean, there's a place for both. Relationships need both."

This isn't a real relationship. I don't want to disagree with her though.

"Business is better when it's planned," I tell her.

"I'm not a businesswoman though."

I nod. "Isn't teaching about planning?"

She squints her eyes at me. "Well, yes, I do have lesson plans, but I also have to be very flexible. Sometimes you have an amazing lesson planned, but there's a fire drill. Or a kid cusses you out and you have to stop what you're doing and fill out a referral. Or, no one understands what you're teaching, and you have to scrap it for a reteach instead."

"That would drive me crazy."

She laughs, a deep, belly laugh that brings tears to her eyes. "I 100 percent see it. I would actually love to see you in the classroom for fifteen minutes."

She laughs some more. I join in. I'd lose my mind.

"Was business always what you wanted to do?" she asks. No woman has ever asked me that before. Not even my mama.

"No."

She's staring at me intently, waiting for more. I've never told anyone more. I've never really let myself admit to more. "I wanted to be a carpenter."

"Sir, you keep acting like you aren't Billionaire Black Jesus, but I'm getting suspicious." She cocks her head to the side, grinning wickedly.

"I mean..." I chuckle and shrug.

"So, what kind of carpentry do you do now?"

"I make all kinds of furniture. If you're free tomorrow morning, I can show you what I've made. What time is your potluck with your friends? That's tomorrow right?

"It's at three. We do it mid-afternoon in case any of us have a date. It's vegan fare. I'm making dessert."

"How do you make dessert without eggs or milk?" I furrow my brows, thinking of ice cream and chocolate cake. Pound cake would be impossible.

"I'm going to alter my sweet potato pie recipe and make it with condensed coconut milk and egg replacer. It'll be an experiment for sure." Her excitement is infectious. I want to make pie with her.

"Save me a slice. I love sweet potato pie."

"I'm making it tonight, so if we meet up tomorrow morning, I will bring you a piece."

"I'll be at the Orchard Harvest farmer's market. I set up at 7:30."

Her eyebrows shoot up. "In the morning?"

I laugh. What farmer's market starts in the evening?

"Yes. 7:30 in the morning. Too early?"

"Well, I try to sleep in, but I can make an exception for you and your carpentry."

It's my turn to be excited. My family doesn't know anything about my permanent booth at the farmer's market. They don't know I make furniture and sell it, giving 100 percent of the profits to charity. My new "girlfriend" will know tomorrow.

***

I arrive at her place in my truck with my trailer attached at seven. I stopped and picked up some coffee for her. There are a few coffee trucks at the farmer's market, but I didn't want to show up empty-handed, especially since I was expecting a piece of her sweet potato pie.

She opens the door with a bright smile. Her weekend outfit is a pair of neon pink yoga pants and an oversized hoodie.

"Oh, you mean business!" she exclaims when she sees my trailer. "And you drove yourself? You're a regular guy right now. I like it!"

"Hey! I am a regular guy. I drive myself a lot." I stop short, realizing having to say that meant the opposite.

"Dru, you are a billionaire. You are not a regular guy, and that is perfectly all right. Now I am a regular girl. I'm a public school teacher who barely makes enough to get by, but I do get by."

"Well, you're my girl now, so you're not regular anymore." I reach out and touch her leg, then quickly withdraw my hand. My subtle touch must've gone unnoticed, because she continues talking like nothing happened.

"Ha! Tell that to my rent and student loans and car payment and my students. Especially my students. They put me through it daily."

"What made you get into teaching?"

"Do you want my stock answer or my real answer?" She's smiling at me, and I can't do anything but smile back.

"I wasn't expecting you to have two. Give me both."

"Okay, so my stock answer is that I've always loved English and literature and reading, and I wanted to instill that into the next generation." I nod. That's a pretty standard response.

"Okay, okay. What's the real answer?"

"The real answer is that I wanted to be a veterinarian, but I'm allergic to dogs and cats, and I couldn't see a way around that, so when my Comp 1 professor told me I was great at writing, I changed my major from biology to English. And the only thing I could think of to be with an English degree is an English teacher." She exhales deeply.

"That sucks, doesn't it?" she asks me.

"It's just sad, I think. You had a dream, and, from how it sounds, not a lot of guidance. You might not have been allergic to horses or cows, and maybe they have allergy shots or something. You switched gears drastically. Are you happy now with your job?"

We have arrived at the Orchard Harvest farmer's market, but I'm enjoying our conversation.

"I'm happy enough. I've found a new passion in preparing seniors for the world, and being able to give them more guidance than I had at their age."

"So, if you had, say $2.5 million, would you keep working?" A sly grin is plastered on my face.

"Hmmm, that's a tough question. I'd take some time off, but eventually, I think I would miss it. I would definitely miss the kids."

"You're so noble," I joke as I open my door. She follows me to the back of the trailer. I fumble with the keys, a little nervous for her to see my work. It's good, but I've never shown it to anyone I interact with regularly like this. I've definitely never shown it to a girlfriend.

"Put me on a magic carpet! This is spectacular! You made all of this?" Her smile is wide as she climbs into the trailer and twists and turns her body through the space to see everything.

"You made a freaking dresser!" she yells from the back of the trailer. I can't help the laugh that bubbles out of me.

She hops out of the trailer, and I pull out the ramp to unload. I notice she is standing right behind me.

"What are you doing?"

"Helping." She looks at me like I just asked the most ridiculous question in the world.

"Oh, I just—no one is ever here to help. I just use my dolly and get it all unloaded myself. I didn't expect you to help."

"Your girlfriend supports your efforts, and she helps you unload your beautiful, handmade furniture out of your trailer." She pushes herself up against me playfully, and I am betrayed by a certain part of my body wanting to play.

"Your boyfriend appreciates the help."

We get the trailer unloaded in half the time. With time left before the market actually opens, I take her to my favorite booths for donuts and more coffee.

Margie and Piper at Glaze and Grind perk up when they see me coming. I know it's because I have Charisse with me. They're always telling me I need to find someone to make my furniture for. I introduce Charisse to them as my girlfriend, and it doesn't feel good to lie, but it's good practice so I can get used to this gross feeling and swallow it down before it shows on my face.

"Finally!" Margie squeals, pulling her glasses off the top of her wild curls to get a better look at Charisse. Margie is an older woman. Her hair is gray, but her spirit is bright. Piper is her teenage granddaughter.

"Miss Turner. You look different outside of school. Is this your rose man?" Piper asks Charisse. My face falls. What are the odds?

"Hey Piper! Yeah, I take my weekends seriously and give myself fashion breaks. I didn't know you and your grandma brought the truck here."

"Yeah, we are out here every weekend. You didn't answer my question. Is this your rose man?"

"Piper, mind your business!" Margie swats at her nosey granddaughter.

"Piper, what if he's not?" Charisse puts her hands on her hips and waits for an answer.

"If he's not, then I just ruined your game. My bad, Miss T."

Charisse howls with laughter. "That's right! You would have, but yes, he is my 'rose man.'" She turns to me. "The roses were a huge distraction. I loved them, but my students are obviously nosey." She waves her hand at Piper who gives a sheepish shrug.

"Noted. No more work roses." I nod my head and make an imaginary check mark in the air.

"Now, I didn't say all that. I still might want to flex on some of the teachers, but not a billion roses. Just a dozen or three." She winks at me.

"Got it. Margie and Piper have the best donuts and coffee at the market. I have tried all of them." I watch Charisse peruse the coffee menu and make googly eyes at all the donuts.

"Get whatever you want. Take whatever you don't eat to your potluck."

"Are these vegan?" she asks.

"No, but they're all delicious," Piper replies.

"Well, I'll take them home for sure, but not to the potluck. If they're as good as you say they are, I won't want to share."

After ordering a caramel macchiato and a dozen assorted donuts, we head back to my booth and get comfortable.

"I cannot believe you made all of this." She is staring behind us at the pop-up furniture store.

"It's my solace. You are actually the first person who knows who I am that I've told."

"Only me? I must be the best girlfriend you've ever had for you to share this with me." She nudges me with her elbow. I smile at her, wondering if she's right.

Chapter 8

Charisse

"Do you want to come in?" I ask Dru at my doorstep.

"Do you have some vegan pie for me?" he says in return, smiling at me with that gorgeous smile of his.

"Oh shoot! Yes I do! I made a whole pie for you. It is delicious! Tastes just like the original!" I open my door and hold it open for him to enter.

"Wait, I almost forgot your end table." He jogs back to the trailer and returns with the end table that is more of a sculpture than furniture. I wouldn't stop talking about how beautiful it was the whole time we were at the farmer's market. When it didn't sell for the $875 he was asking for, Dru said I could have it. Making that extra pie was serendipitous. I have something to give him in return.

"Do you want a piece right now?"

"Yes ma'am!" The twinkle of anticipation in his eyes makes me smile."Where do I put this?" he asks. The end table is heavy, and I get distracted watching his muscles flex as he holds it.

"Oh, um, right in the middle of the living room. It'll be my teeny tiny coffee table. I have been meaning to get one, but the ones

I love are too expensive. Porsche dogs me out every time she comes over here."

"I have a whole trailer, well half a trailer full of furniture. Is there anything else in there you want?" He moves toward my front door.

"No, you already gave me this very expensive end table. That's enough for one day. I'll milk you during our engagement." I laugh and wink at him. "Come sit down and have some pie with me. I'm eating some too. When we're married, I will make you a pie every week."

"The same pie?" He takes a bite and moans. The hairs on the back of my neck stand up. I'll make him pie every day if he keeps making those sounds. I force myself to breathe before I take a bite.

"Please make this for me every week forever. I may need to marry you for real over this pie." He continues to moan with each bite, and I have to cross my legs tightly to keep myself under control.

"We will just have to see about that." I wink at him. "Do you cook at all?"

"No. I get too wrapped up in following recipes exactly, and I've come to find out cooking is a lot about instincts. Pinches of this and sprinkles of that. I prefer things to be exact."

"I'm catching that." He's wrapped up a little tight. "Outside of carpentry, what do you do to relax? What do you do for fun?"

He looks lost and confused.

"Oh, so your mom is right, and you are married to your job. You'll never actually settle down, will you?"

"I've been focused on business since I was in high school. I don't know anything else."

"When was your last serious relationship?"

"The family business means everything to me. My mom started it, and I want it to be passed down through generations. I feel this immense responsibility to keep it thriving. I don't know how to qualify a relationship as serious, but no one has come before my business."

I listen intently, sensing the weight of his words. "I can understand how important that is to you, Dru. Building and preserving a legacy can be fulfilling. But have you ever thought about what else life has to offer? Relationships, companionship, love…those are the things that truly enrich our lives. Those are reasons for living.""

Dru's gaze shifts, his eyes momentarily clouded with doubt. "I suppose I've always believed that success is measured by how much you've achieved in your professional life."

I sit down on the couch, motioning for him to join me. "There is more than that, Dru. Life is about balance. It's about finding joy not just in work, but in the connections we forge, the relationships we build. Our loved ones are the ones who truly make us feel alive."

He lets out a contemplative sigh, his fingers tracing the rim of his pie plate. "I never really had the time for dating, or maybe I never allowed myself to make the time. I've been so consumed by the family business, always striving for success."

I reach out, gently placing a hand on his arm. "Dru, I don't doubt your dedication and hard work. Life is meant to be lived. Money and success are important, but they're not the sole measure of a fulfilling life. You can't leave a legacy if you don't have other people to share it with. And why have a billion dollars just sitting in the bank? You don't vacation either, do you?"

He chuckles. "Nope. I work and work, then work some more." He runs his hand down his face.

"Are you," I pause, trying to decide if I should ask this question or not. "Are you a virgin?"

He howls with laughter. "No! I make time for that."

"But no relationships?" I feel that Kerry Washington expression crawling across my face. He could at least lie to me. Damn.

"Hey, a man has needs." He shrugs.

"Physical needs only? Do you even have friends?" I cock my head to the side and raise my eyebrows.

"Are you judging me?" There's a heart-melting smile on his face that loosens up my scowl.

"Yes I am," I say, returning the smile. I have so many questions that I'm not sure I'm allowed to ask. I don't think there was anything in the contract about getting to know him deeply.

"Let's change the subject. What about you?" He crosses his arms over his chest and stares at me.

"I've had four serious relationships." And four devastating heartbreaks. I want this conversation to end now.

"Tell me about the last one, if you don't mind." He leans closer to me. Something about him makes me bare my soul to him.

"His name was Valentino."

"Valentino!" He laughs with his whole body.

"It seemed cool and exotic at the time, but he was just toxic."

He regained his composure. "Continue."

I roll my eyes at him and slap his thigh. "Anyway, he initially swept me off my feet. He took me out all the time. Had me neglecting my girls and spending every extra moment with him. I was caught up. So excited that this man wanted all of my time. I felt so loved and adored. But that shit was a lie." A chill ran through my body as I remember the day I came to my senses with Valentino.

"All he wanted was to control you?" Dru asks. I nod, trying to stuff that memory deep down.

I wrap the pie in foil and hand it to him at my door. He leans in and kisses me on the cheek—an unscheduled kiss.

"Today was the most fun I've had in a while. Thank you."

I feel my face flush, but I smile at him anyway and tell him goodbye. I close my door and lean against it. His lips were soft like I thought they would be, but I didn't know they'd be that soft.

I put my hand up to my cheek and wonder what this unscheduled kiss means. Was it just a friendly gesture? Was it more?

***

"Oooh, I love this table. Where'd you get it from? It's too small to be a coffee table, but it's a start."

Porsche surveys my new living room arrangement, focusing on the table Dru made.

"My boyfriend gave it to me."

"That's random. He just gave you a single end table? Not even a set?"

I giggle. Porsche can't help being judgmental. She's a libra.

"Porsche, he made it. I have so much to tell you and Lily. Where is she?"

"I don't know. I called her before I left, and she didn't answer."

"Maybe she got caught up at the studio. I'll text her right quick."

I pull up our message thread and start typing out a text.

"Sorry y'all! I'm here. I fell asleep. That never happens. I've been so busy lately." Lily stands in my door holding her matching travel dishes. I'm scared. Lily thinks she can cook, but it is usually hit or miss. Porsche and I will never say a word to her about it. We've never actually said anything about it to each other, but we have silent conversations about her food every single week. She once made pot roast in the pressure cooker. The looks we exchanged when she asked us for a knife to cut into it could have been memes. Everyone knows if you have to cut pot roast, then it's no good.

"Cute table. Where'd you get it from?"

I laugh and take Lily's travel dishes to set out on my counter. "Let's get some food first. There's so much to tell you."

With plates full of food—I always get a tiny taste of whatever Lily's made, then I go back for fake seconds and throw serving spoonfuls into the garbage disposal so she won't think we didn't like it—we settle at the dining table and eat.

"So, spill it," Porsche demands.

I consider being coy, but I can't. "He's nice. A really nice guy."

"That's what you had to tell us?" Porsche rolls her eyes. "I thought you got the goods. Did the do. This isn't exciting."

Lily looks at me and nods, agreeing with Porsche.

"I really had a great day with him, and this is going to be an easy way to make this money is all I'm saying. He's kind and interesting."

"So." Lily wags her fork at me. "What you're saying is that you will end up falling in love with him? Our best friend is going to be the real wife to a billionaire." Lily clinks her fork with Porsche's, and I roll my eyes.

"She's not," I say. "He's very sterile. He plans everything. You saw the schedule he made. I don't see him being adventurous or spontaneous. He's a robot."

Porsche and Lily exchange looks. "She's trying to make him sound awful. Oh he's so terrible. He plans everything and communicates well and is the picture of stability. Girl hush!" Porsche mocks me and bursts into laughter, slapping her thigh, Lily's thigh, and the table.

"It's not that funny." I frown. "He's boring. Nice and kind, but he's boring. I can't live my whole life with someone boring. But I can do seventeen months. For sure. Seventeen months for $2.5 million."

"Keep telling yourself that," Porsche says with a mouth full of pie.

Chapter 9

Dru

Skyline doesn't have a single empty table tonight. My schedule notes that I need to take at least three selfies with Charisse tonight to post on social media. Our farmer's market post from last week got a lot of traction. My brothers seemed to ignore her roses post, but my photos immediately had Draymond on the phone with me, their twin telepathy kicking in at the same time. Draymond called me first, and Drummond called thirty seconds later.

"Who is that fine ass woman?" Draymond demands, not greeting me at all. I laugh, and before I could reply, Drummond called. I added him in and let them tag-team interrogate me about Charisse. My spreadsheet of information sat ready on the tablet in front of me on my desk.

"My new girl. Mom thinks she knows everything about me, but she doesn't. This one is special, and I've kept her close." The lie was velvety—felt good coming out.

"Since when do you keep anything close?" Drummond asks. I know the exact expression he had on his face. He isn't buying it at all.

"Since I found Charisse." There is something about her. I keep that to myself to unpack later.

"Bro, she's fine. If you're happy, then I'm happy. She's real into you too. She's got that twinkle in her eyes in the pictures. I looked at her other pictures on socials, and that twinkle is only there when she's in pictures with you." Draymond's voice starts getting that preaching cadence. I have to cut the conversation.

"All right. All right. You will meet her eventually. I'm about to link up with her now, so I gotta go." I end the call before they can add anything else. I don't need them prying any further.

"Mr. Martin, what are you and the lady drinking tonight?" The waiter asks. I look toward Charisse with my eyebrows raised.

"Any ideas?"

She smiles at me, and something in my chest tightens. I clear my throat and look away.

"Surprise me," she tells the waiter.

Watching her lean into this wealthy lifestyle makes me smile. She revels in it, but I can tell she's trying hard to not take advantage...like she could do that at all.

"You didn't always have money?" she asks me after the waiter steps away. The yellow of her jumper really pops against her skin. A Black girl in yellow is one of my weaknesses.

"You look so good in that outfit." It slips out of my mouth. She needs to know though.

She looks down at herself and up at me. "Thank you. Should we get the waiter to take our picture when he gets back? A full-length picture. I do look very good today. Might as well show it off." She winks at me, and I find myself needing the waiter to take a little longer because standing up would show her how hard she's got me.

Shit! This isn't supposed to happen. I did pick a beautiful woman to get fake married to, but I'm not actually supposed to like her.

"Yeah, let's ask before we eat because I heard this place is on point, and I don't want to have a photo of either of us with the 'itis by the end of our date."

She throws her head back and howls with laughter, exposing the smooth skin of her neck to me. How would it feel to kiss her neck? I grab my phone off the table and snap a quick photo of her laughing and post the photo. The world needs to see how pretty my girl is.

My fake girl.

"To answer your question, no. My mom started the company when I was in middle school. The twins and Dreya were in high school. She and Pops missed all of my football games and basketball games after they started the company. I understood though. My games were a blip on the radar when they were building what is now a billion dollar company." I shrug, trying to shake away the sad eighth grader who made ten three-pointers in one game and had no one there to cheer him on.

"I quit sports my senior year, knowing it wasn't the direction anyone wanted me to go in." I glance at Charisse, and her eyes are full of empathy.

"Was it the direction you wanted to go in?" Her attention focuses on me. No one asks me questions like this. They only ask about how I spend my money or how I make my money. Most people don't delve deep with me.

"Don't all Black boys who play sports want to go pro at some point in their lives?" I ask, sheepishly, embarrassed to be a stereotype.

Charisse releases another laugh that clinches around my heart and makes me laugh too. "They all do, don't they?"

"What did you major in your freshman year? It's not what degree you graduated with, is it?"

It's my turn to burst into laughter. How'd she know that?

"No, I majored in biology when I first started school."

Her eyes light up. "Really?!"

"Figured I'd be a doctor. I didn't have any real passion for it, but it's another one of those things. Saying I'm going to be a doctor sounds great to parents and their friends."

"How interesting that we both started that way." Her eyes are thoughtful. I'm anxious to hear her next question.

"Hey, Dru! I didn't expect to see you here!"

I turn around and Draymond stands behind me, all smiles and peering eyes. Charisse isn't supposed to meet my family for another week, at the least. My hands clench on the table, and Charisse reaches out to hold one of them, instantly relaxing me. We make eye contact, and her smile lets me know she's got this.

"Draymond, hey! It's so packed in here, I'm surprised I haven't run into the whole family. Who are you here with?"

"Some work buddies. The real question is who are you here with?" He reaches his hand out to Charisse. "I'm Draymond, the handsomest of the Martin brothers."

"Aren't you and Drummond identical?" Charisse asks, teasing.

I didn't know she knew anything about them. I'd planned to talk about families tonight actually. A quick internet search of our family gave her that information though. I'm grateful.

"Everything about us isn't identical." He grins, and I'm about to punch him in the face.

"You sound like a predator," Charisse tells him, a look of disgust on her face.

"Whoa! I'm half a centimeter taller than him, and I have a mole on my left cheek while Drummond has one on his right. Y'all nasty."

Charisse cackles, tears stream down her face, and she's holding her stomach.

"You two are perfect for each other. Damn. Both jumping the Grand Canyon with conclusions." Draymond shakes his head.

"Shut up. This is my girlfriend, Charisse. Charisse, my older brother Draymond."

"The handsomest of the Martin brothers," he repeats.

"It's nice to meet you, Draymond, left-cheek moled twin."

The waiter approaches with our drinks, and Draymond gives us both his goofiest grin and heads back to his table. We place our orders with the waiter before resuming our conversation.

"That was awkward." I sigh, taking a big gulp of my drink.

"No, it was hilarious and classic big brother antics." She leans in close to me and whispers, "You're the handsomest Martin brother."

I feel my face heat up, but red rarely shows on my skin. "Well thank you."

"How was school today?"

"Oooh," she laughs. "That's a real couple question." Somehow our chairs are closer together at the corner of the small, square table. She nudges my elbow with hers.

"Oh yeah? Well, I'm actually curious. High school is a foreign country to me. I see stuff about it on social media with kids acting crazy on teachers, but I have no idea about the day to day." I don't add that I went to a prestigious, private high school.

"It was a nice day. Once a week, we do a real-world activity, so today they filled out three job applications and did mock interviews."

I don't tell her that I've never filled out a job application or been interviewed for a job.

"How about you?" she asks. "How was your day?" Charisse sips her bright pink drink and shimmies.

"Delicious or too strong?" I laugh as she places the glass back on the table.

"Yes, both. Mostly it is delicious. The waiter didn't tell us what these drinks are. Oh well, tell me about your day."

I don't really want to get into business acquisition and the issues I'm having over the small details. That'll just bore her, so I pause to consider what to say.

"Don't give me a stock answer Dru Martin. Tell me what your day was like. I actually want to know."

"I love that you want to know, but it really was a boring day. Do you mind talking about our families? You meeting Draymond today makes it even more important. You can google my family and get some information, but I know nothing about yours."

A wisp of disappointment flashes across her face, but she recovers and nods in agreement with me.

"There's not much to tell though. It's pretty boring too. My parents split up when I was in tenth grade and my baby sister was in eighth grade. My mom had primary custody, and we saw my dad on weekends and for a month during the summer." She shrugs like she didn't just rattle off, in my eyes, an atypical family dynamic.

"How was it when your parents divorced? Did you and your sister take it hard?" I can't imagine my parents not being together.

"They'd started being weird with each other a few years before. They didn't think I noticed, but I did. They didn't fight or anything, but they just stopped being cool with each other, you know? No touching. No kissing. Not really spending time together."

"Do you know why? Did they ever talk to you?" One thing about my parents I admire is their communication. They still include us in all major decisions. Their door's always open.

"My parents are old school. Everything happened because they said so. Neither of them tolerated back talk. My mom hated being questioned about anything. She expected us to accept everything she said and did as law: no questions asked." She frowns then looks up at me and smiles. "I don't want to be that kind of parent. I think some parts of our childhood are there to teach us what not to do in the future. I try my best not to be bitter, but it seeps out sometimes. I don't like dealing with her that much." A sadness takes over her eyes.

I reach out and take her hand, giving it a gentle squeeze. She squeezes back, and we sit in silence for a few moments.

The waiter arrives with our food, and we get lost in our meals.

Charisse eats half of her food before she utters another word.

"This is so good!" she says, her mouth full. "Do you want to taste it?" She offers her fork to me, and it looks too delicious to resist.

"Damn, that is good. It's better than mine, and mine is delicious." I extend my fork to her, and she leans forward. Her lips wrap around my fork, and I lose myself for a minute, wondering how they'd feel on mine. I clear my throat and put my fork back on my plate.

"Should we get our stories straight?" she asks, taking a final sip of her drink. Her now warm face glows in the low light of the dining room, and I can't think. I want to touch her soft brown skin.

I slam my eyes shut to stop from looking at her. I probably look crazy, so I rub my eyes, feigning exhaustion or allergies or anything other than accepting how attracted I am to this woman.

"Uh, yeah," I reply, much delayed. "That's a great idea."

"Let's start with how we met. I've been thinking about this, and we can just tell the truth. We met at the paint and sip. Our revisionist story will be that you got my number there, and boom, we connected." Her smile beams.

"I did go there to meet women," I admit. "I just forgot to actually make an attempt to do that. You and Porsche were the only women I spoke to, and I didn't even get your number." I want to kick myself because I could really be dating this woman. She is magnificent, but she's here only for the money I offered.

It feels like there is a vise in my chest. I think I've found someone special, but I've screwed it up by proposing to her with money and an expiration date instead of with love and a ring.

Chapter 10

Charisse

I have been eating so well lately. Dru and I have been on a handful of dates these past two weeks. We've been doing a tour of the most popular and expensive restaurants in town, and I've never eaten food so decadent and delicious. I'm loving this lifestyle—and the time I'm spending with Dru. He's so unexpected. When he told me he was just a regular guy, I couldn't comprehend how that could be, but he is down to earth and funny, even if he constantly posts about us on social media and schedules our fake life almost down to the minute.

I pull up his schedule on my phone and laughter bubbles up. He has a reminder that we will be getting engaged within the next two weeks. I won't let him tell me the exact date. It's fun to push his buttons, but the man needs to balance his schedule with a little intrigue or spontaneity. This thing we're doing isn't real, but it can be fun.

While I'm looking at our plans for this week, my phone rings and scares me so badly that I drop it on the pile of papers I'm supposed to be grading. My sister's name flashes on the screen.

"This is weird," I say before tapping the phone to answer it. "Hey Yanique!" I add some syrup to my voice. I love my sister, but I don't really like her that much. We've never been close, and as we get older, we grow further and further apart. We're both probably to blame for not making the effort.

"Hey 'Risse! What are you doing?" She sounds so chipper—almost excited.

I pull the phone away from my face and look at it. My sister's tone with me is always bored and dry. Who is this?

"I'm grading papers. The never-ending task."

"You're too smart to be a teacher. I don't know why you didn't try to do something that made you some money." She always tells me that. And she always gives me compliments wrapped in insults.

I don't respond, letting the silence get awkward.

"Soooo, I'm getting married," she says with just the slightest hilt in her voice. I can tell she wants to have a moment with me, but my throat is bone dry now. I'm getting married soon. Will this look weird? Will I look like I'm trying to one-up her or be just like her?

"Congratulations! Who is your fiancé? I didn't realize you were dating someone." I think I regained my composure quite nicely.

"Oh, you don't know anything about me these days." She laughs. "He's a mechanical engineer, and his name is Byron."

It's not lost on me that she introduced me to his profession before his name. And Byron? He sounds nerdy.

"Amazing! That's great news. I'm happy for you! When did you get engaged?" I know I have to ask all the right questions to make her feel seen.

"Last week..."

I put the phone on the table in front of me and clench my fists. Why the hell did she wait a whole week to tell me? I'm the oldest in the family, not some random stray they picked up off the road. My phone number hasn't changed since I got my phone in high school.

I release my hands and pick the phone back up. She never noticed I wasn't there and is going on about the car Byron drives: a McLaren which does not scream DBE to me, but what do I know?

"Oh wow," I interject here and there to show her my amazement.

When she seems to be winding down, I ask when the wedding will be.

"Oh, probably around this time next year. There's so much to plan, expenses to figure out. Weddings are productions. It takes time to do it right."

I almost laugh. I'll have a month to plan an extravagant wedding. There'll be no expenses to figure out. Part of me can't wait to blow her mind with my fake wedding, but the unpetty part of me wants to be happy for her. I don't know why I'm not.

"What about an engagement party? Are you having one of those?" I don't know why I keep asking questions instead of getting off the phone.

"Yeah, I'm working on the guest list right now. You'll make it, right?"

"Of course. When is it?" We live about an hour away from one another, so why wouldn't I make it?

"I'm not sure. Probably in a few months though. I have to coordinate with Mom and Dad and my real dad too."

My head cocks to the side. Her real dad?

"Your real dad?" I repeat, wondering if she's had some kind of stroke or mental break.

"Um, Mom didn't ever tell you?" she asks, genuine curiosity in her voice.

"Yanique, Mom didn't ever tell me what?" I'm trying to keep my voice down, but I want to scream right now.

"Dad isn't my biological dad. Mom cheated on him and got pregnant with me. She hid it from Dad until the year before their divorce. Dad tried to keep the family together, so he didn't leave her when he first found out, but he couldn't stay. Wow, I can't believe Mom didn't tell you." Her voice is so nonchalant, like she didn't just blow up everything I thought was my childhood.

"How long have you known this?" I ask through gritted teeth. My eyes are closed, and I've laid down on my couch like I'm in a therapist's office.

"Um, two years I think. Yeah, two years. I found out who he was last year, and you're not going to believe it."

What the hell is happening? Did I get dismissed from the family and not get the memo? Two years?

"Who is it?" Why not get all the info now so I can wallow in all of it later.

"Are you sure you're ready?" she asks, like a little kid. I want to tell her to cut the bullshit.

"It's Uncle Lamar." She squeals with laughter.

"Are you fucking serious?" I scream. Everything is a lie. I am so disgusted and sad.

"I know." She giggles. "Mom was boning Uncle Lamar. So gross, but he's really cool, and now I have two dads." She sounds so bubbly, like she didn't just drop the biggest bomb on me.

"Yeah, you sure do." My voice is dry and dull. "Oop, my phone is about to—" I hang up on her and curl into a ball on my couch. My instincts usually have me calling my girls, but I want to hear Dru's voice instead. I can already hear Porsche and Lily. Both will have distinct reactions and approaches to this. Porsche will have a fuck them all attitude, and Lily will try to understand; she'll encourage me to ask questions and to forgive for the sake of family and my sanity. I don't want to hear either of those right now.

"Hey," I say, my voice shaky and uneven.

"What's wrong?" he says with so much alarm in his voice I almost feel bad for calling him.

"Family stuff. Everyone's okay, but—"

"I'll be there in fifteen minutes. Do you want me to stay on the phone until I get there?" he asks.

I can hear his keys jingling. He's dropping everything for me.

"Uh, no. I'll just wait for you to get here."

Fifteen minutes later, he knocks on my door. I skip the quick look in the mirror, knowing how terrible I look, but not caring. When I open the door, he's standing there holding Chinese takeout and wearing gray sweatpants. Did he come to cheer me up with more than food and hugs?

I keep my eyes on his face because I'm dying to look at his print. I just know this man is packing. Not that it matters though, because we won't be consummating our marriage. Still, I can be curious, can't I?

"What happened?" he asks, staring into my eyes.

I got distracted thinking about his junk. I forgot I was actually upset. I hesitate, feeling silly for having him come all the way over here for my family drama. He's not my real boyfriend. Why'd I do that?

He never takes his eyes off me. I feel comforted and not exposed or awkward. I tell him everything I just found out from my sister.

"That's fucked up." He doesn't say anything else. What else is there to say? It is fucked up.

"I know," I begin. "My mom cheating on my dad is one thing. But them knowing, and spilling it all to each other and leaving me out? That's the most fucked up part."

"The secret baby with the uncle is pretty…"

"Ratchet." I finish his sentence.

"Well, yes. It's admirable that your dad tried to stick around. I don't know if i could do that."

I stare at him then pinch the bridge of my nose. He's not understanding my frustration. My rage. He's looking at the big picture instead of the details, which is frustrating as hell given that he's neurotic about details.

"Dru, fuck my dad's admirable qualities. My whole fucking

family kept this huge secret from me. My sister is only my half sister. They had a whole conversation...a whole family fucking meeting probably, and they left me out." I will myself not to cry. They don't deserve my tears.

"I'm sorry. I'm just processing it all out loud. I can't comprehend leaving you out of it. That's bullshit, Charisse. Pure bullshit." He stares at me with his dark brown eyes, pools of darkness that seem to see the core of me.

"It is bullshit. You know, I felt a little bad about lying to them about us, but my fake marriage to you is nothing compared to this. I almost don't want to invite them at all. But that'll raise suspicions with your family." I sigh. Dru wraps his arm around me and leads me to my couch. I didn't even let the man sit down before I unloaded on him.

I feel very exposed now, very vulnerable and even silly because this is none of his concern. I avoid eye contact and pull away from him. "I'm sorry I made you come all this way for my family's drama. It's none of your concern, and I just interrupted your evening with it."

His arm snakes its way around me again. "You didn't make me do anything. I got in the car the moment I heard the sadness in your voice. It was my choice. And I'm happy you called me. I might not be your real boyfriend, but I think we're becoming friends."

I still can't make eye contact with him, and he seems to understand.

"I'm going to head out, but if you need to talk, I'll be a phone call away," he tells me as he places the softest kiss on my forehead.

I open my eyes as he kisses me and catch a glimpse of his monstrous print. It's so big it takes my breath away.

"Th-th-thank you," I manage to say as he makes his way to the door. I still can't look at him, but now it's for a completely different reason.

"Any time."

I moan a little when he closes the door. I wouldn't know what to do with him, but I'd love to figure it out.

I'm not even upset anymore, but I don't understand why they wouldn't tell me. Although, it's not quite my business when I really get down to it. It doesn't involve me at all.

Maybe that's why Yanique and I have never been close. We're only half siblings. No. I've seen step siblings with more chemistry than my sister and I have.

I shake my head, trying to free my mind of these random thoughts: family drama and dick prints. I need to get it together. Now's not the time to think about this. I have papers to grade.

Chapter 11

Charisse

"I want you to meet my mom," Dru says, casually dropping a boulder on me in the middle of dinner at The Sapphire. Running into one of his brothers is one thing. Officially meeting his mother is quite another, and I'm not ready for this at all.

"Why?" It comes out before I know I'm asking. I clear my throat. "I mean...well, why right now?" There's no way around the question; I need to know his reason.

"We're getting engaged next week, and I feel like it would be respectful to her for me to introduce the two of you before I pop the question." He takes a bite of his salad and stares at me.

His logic always hits just right. I frown into my glass of water. I need wine immediately, so I twist and look behind me for the waiter. As soon as we make eye contact, he's by my side.

"What can I get for you?" he asks.

"A bottle of wine, please. Something sweet and fruity."

Dru laughs. "Sweet and fruity, eh? You're not a connoisseur?"

"Nope, especially not when I'm trying to drink my anxiety away." I hold my glass up for the waiter to pour my first of many glasses of wine. Then I take a deep swig. It's perfect.

"This is delicious! What is it?" The waiter heads to the table with the bottle, but Dru waves him off.

"I'll have a case sent to you in the morning. You're avoiding my request." He grins and looks my way.

I hide behind my glass of wine. "Yes, I am."

"Why?" he asks me, like he's not asking me to meet his billionaire, CEO mother. She's going to think I'm a gold-digger who's only marrying her son for money.

Shit. She's going to be right.

"I don't think we can be convincing. Mothers know, and she'll be able to see that we're faking from a mile away. It's going to ruin everything." I chug my wine and look toward our waiter. He hurries to my side and refills my glass.

Dru pulls his chair close to mine and leans in, our mouths just centimeters apart. He turns his head and breathes in my scent and brushes his lips along my neck, making me shudder from his touch. "I think we will be convincing enough," he whispers in my ear.

He distracts me for a moment, but my mind races. She's going to figure us out instantly. She knows her son. My throat goes dry, and I pick up my wine glass only to discover it's empty yet again.

"You have water right here," Dru reminds me, pushing my glass of water closer to me.

I cut my eyes at him. My favorite waiter in the whole world reappears, and my glass is filled to the top yet again.

"Leave him an amazing tip," I tell Dru. I sip on this glass of wine. My brain's starting to get cloudy, and the room's tilted. I feel my body sway.

"You're drunk." Dru laughs. "This is new."

"Are you enjoying it?" I ask, my words slurring.

"I don't hate it," he says.

"Why not?" I try to shift in my seat, and I end up falling into his lap. He catches me with his powerful arms and sets me upright. "Oooh, you're so strong. You just blooped me back in my seat. I'm not tiny at all, and you did that without any effort." I trail my hand down his bicep. He flexes his arm for me, and I squeal.

"Because you're unfiltered. You aren't trying to say or do the right thing. I like it." He rests his hand on mine and looks into my eyes.

I hiccup and lean into his body. "Maybe I need to be drunk when I meet your mom."

"Oh, no. That's a bad idea. She's a little uptight about that kind of thing."

"Tell me about her. Do you like her?"

"Do I like her?" he repeats.

"Yeah, it says a lot about a mother if her children still want to be around her when they don't have to anymore. Trust me, I learned psychology on socials." I give him a matter-of-fact nod that makes me sway again. He puts an arm around me to keep me upright.

"I like her enough then, I guess. I don't have any childhood traumas that make me dislike her. I wish she'd made it to more of my activities when I was a kid, but she was building an empire, and that requires sacrifice."

"You were the sacrifice?" I ask. He's right. My filter left a long time ago.

"I wouldn't say that..." He pauses, and I focus on the adorable mole I just discovered on his jawline.

"Maybe I was the sacrifice," he says, his brows furrowed.

"Was it worth it for you?"

"Damn, are you sure you didn't get a degree in psychotherapy in real life?" he asks, obviously trying to evade my question.

"Nope, just on socials. You didn't answer my question, by the way." I wag my finger in his face.

"What was the question again?" A sly smile spreads across his face.

I purse my lips and cock my head to the side. What was my question?

"Oh, you're lucky I'm drunk. I can't remember."

My buzz wears off the moment Chance pulls up to my apartment. Dru told me we'd meet his mother in two days. I stumble to the bathroom, feeling sick to my stomach. Slumping on the floor next to the toilet, I realize I'm sick from nerves, not wine. I never get sick from alcohol.

I don't know how to navigate this. I open the video chat app on my phone and call my girls.

"You look like shit," Porsche tells me upon seeing my face on the screen.

"As I should."

"What happened?" Lily asks. "Did Dru break up with you?"
I laugh. That man's not breaking up our fake, contractual relationship.

"Worse, he wants me to meet his mom, THE Madeline Martin."
I lay back and rest my head on the edge of the bathtub. It's cool porcelain zaps a bit of energy into my body.

"Oh shit. That's a real test. How are you going to fake it with his mom? She has to be good at reading people since she's a freaking mogul," Porsche asks.

"I know. That's why I'm so stressed. She's going to see right through us. Or, she'll think I'm some gold-digger after her son's money."

"That's not untrue," Lily says, making a face. She's still not okay with this situation.

"HE approached ME. I didn't learn who he was and chase him down. His lawyer drew up the contracts."

Lily looks away and stays quiet. I huff and pinch the bridge of my nose.

"You just need a game plan. Figure some things out about her, and be yourself when you meet her. You can do this, Friend!"

"He wants me to meet his family!" I squawk.

"What are you going to do?" Lily asks.

"I'm going to go. I can't avoid it." I shrug. Fear coursing through my blood.

"You know what?" Porsche begins. "You'll be so nervous from worrying about fooling her that she'll figure it's nerves from meeting her. Don't put another thought into it. Just go be your nervous, clumsy self."

"Excuse me?" I glare at her through the screen.

"You know you get clumsy when you're super nervous. Don't go in that woman's luxury apartment and break some priceless vase."

Lily laughs so much she snorts. "Remember that time you fell into Brandon's father's lap—face first into his junk?"

Porsche joins her in reliving my most humiliating dating moment. I had to break up with Brandon after that. Faceplanting on his dad's junk was the ruin of our relationship. It was that day I learned his lack of size was genetic.

"You two are no help." I giggle. I can laugh about it now, but it was absolutely horrifying. His dad threw me off him like I was his mistress, and his wife had just walked in. His wife glared at me like I was trying to get at her husband and her son. I had to disappear on him. I blocked his number and never went back to the coffee shop we'd frequent. Luckily, it was closer to his place than it was to mine.

"What are you wearing?" Porsche asks, changing the subject and adding on to my anxiety.

"Fuck! What should I wear? A business suit? A cute dress? Casual jeans?" I rush to my closet and slide hangers back and forth.

"Whatever you do, don't wear one of your teacher outfits."

Porsche says, eyeballing me.

"What? What's wrong with my teacher outfits? They're appropriate for all ages," I tell her, feeling offended.

"They're boring," Lily answers for her, shrugging. "Some of them are frumpy, and she'll think you're a poor teacher who's marrying her son for money."

"Damn. Th—"

Porsche interrupts me. "Yes, that is what you're doing, but she doesn't need to know that. If you can't at least feel like his girlfriend, then you can look a little more sophisticated."

"You're both bitches."

"Bitches who have your best interest at heart. Have that man take you shopping," Porsche tells me.

"No, have him send a car for us and foot the bill when we take you shopping," Lily adds

"Hell yeah!" Porsche yells.

I feel better when we end the call. I'll at least not look terrible when I meet Dru's mother. I send him a text asking him about a mini shopping spree. He answers immediately asking when and where and if $2,500 is enough.

I drop the phone. When I pick it up, I call him.

"That's almost my whole paycheck for a month," I say the moment he answers the phone.

"Seriously? That's bullshit." He's typing on his phone.

"I'm interrupting you. I'm sorry. I'll let you go." I perch my finger above the end call button on my screen.

"No, check your account. I just sent you $5,000. Go crazy!"

"You just what?" I ask as I open my banking app and see the deposit. "Holy shit," I whisper.

"Buy something for meeting my mom. Buy some new dresses

for our next few dates. And buy something for your sister's engagement party."

Chapter 12

Charisse

Dru's rushing out of the elevator. I think he's forgotten that I'm with him. "Dru!" I whisper, tugging on his arm. I shouldn't have listened to Porsche when she made me buy these heels. They're gorgeous and not even that high, but I'm not used to walking in them.

"Oh, sorry," he says as he reaches back for my hand. I shuffle up to him, and we walk slowly into the foyer of her luxury apartment.

I remind myself that gawking at the opulence around me won't help my chances of impressing her. I still take in the sights. Vases full of flowers are everywhere. Dahlias and lilies are the most prominent. I smile, happy that roses aren't dominating. She has these flowers here because she delights in them, not for show.

There's a lot of show here though. The hardwood floors shine as if they're polished daily. It's interesting that she has hardwood instead of marble or tile. It feels comfortable.

The wall of family portraits stops me in my tracks. I let go of Dru's hand and examine each photo one by one. His sister is jaw-dropping gorgeous. And she has a baby. I squeal when I see her photo.

"I react the same way when I see Jurnee too," a soft voice says right next to me.

Dru's mother stands beside me, a warm smile on her face as she looks at her children and granddaughter on the wall.

"You have a beautiful family, Mrs. Martin," I say before I turn to her and give her a warm smile. She smiles back at me.

"I'm Charisse," I tell her as I extend my hand.

She pulls me into a hug. "It's so nice to meet you."

That's not what I was expecting. She's supposed to be cold and businesslike. She's giving me a mom hug.

It takes me a beat to put my arms around her and return the embrace.

"Dru hasn't told me a single thing about you, so we have so much to talk about today." She keeps her hands on my arms and smiles at me. "Let's go sit down and have some tea."

She's gentle and sweet. I'm having a hard time processing this. I scan the room for Dru. He's at the bar area making himself a drink.

"What are you nervous about, Dru?" I ask. "I'm the one about to be in the hot seat."

His mother laughs, and Dru freezes, slowly turning to face us both. The look on his face mirrors how I feel: confused. He sets his glass down and joins us in the sitting room. Madeline sits in the oversized chair while Dru and I sit beside each other on the couch.

"Where do we start?" Madeline says, clasping her hands together

86

in her lap.

"I suppose we start at the beginning," Dru says. We plotted out the story of how we met last night. There's not much fabrication. We did meet at the paint and sip, but we're adding that we exchanged numbers and texted all night.

"A paint and sip?" Madeline asks.

"It's where people get together to create a painting with an instructor. One of my best friends does them every weekend. She's doing so well with it. I think she's making as much with her pop-ups as she is with her day job." I don't know why I'm telling his mother Lily's business like this.

"Well, don't tell her to quit her day job just yet. She needs to keep doing both and investing into her business with the money her business makes her," Madeline tells me as she pours herself some tea.

"Thanks. I will."

"What about you? What's your story?" She takes a dainty sip of her tea.

"Well, I'm just a high school teacher." I hate answering this question.

"Just? You aren't just a high school teacher. Your job doesn't determine who you are. I want to know you, not what you do." Her eyes meet mine. I hadn't rehearsed my answer to this question.

"Well." I clear my throat to buy time. "I'm not that close to my family, to be honest. I wish I was. I have two of the best friends anyone could ask for who help balance me out. I love to read—I'm an English teacher, and that just comes with the territory.

I'm passionate about helping young people reach their potential because no one was there to help me reach mine."

Dru gives my hand a squeeze, and Madeline nods then lays into her next question. "What do you see in my son...other than his bank account?"

I'm mid-sip of my tea, and I end up choking on it, which sends me into a coughing fit. I gag and gasp for air for an eternity before my airways clear.

"I didn't mean to startle you, Charisse. Are you okay?" Madeline asks, her face now void of expression.

"Yes, I'm fine. I just wasn't expecting that last part of your question. I didn't know who Dru was when I first met him," I begin. It's true, so it comes out easy. "That night we texted until dawn almost, and it was his personality and his wit that made me want to go on a date with him. I was impressed he could get us into The Sapphire on such short notice, but by the time I learned about you and the Martin empire, I was already pretty deep in my feelings for him." I turn to Dru. "He's a spectacular human being with such talent for the things he's passionate about. I find his need to plan out everything endearing, but he knows I like surprises too, and he showers me with a good mix of who he is and what I like. I'm with him because he's kind and fun and caring. Not because he's rich."

I sigh and squeeze Dru's hand back. I'm sure she's used to women flocking to her sons and only being after the money. While I'm with Dru for the money, I didn't flock to him. This deception was all his idea.

Madeline nods at me again and assesses me.

"Mom," Dru says, with some authority in his voice. I turn to him, and I have to stop the tug at the corners of my mouth. I like that tone on him. I place my hand on his leg and scoot a little closer to him. He wraps his arm around my body and rests his hand on my hip. I revel in the feel of him, forgetting where I am until his mother speaks again.

"I don't mean any offense. You boys don't always think with your brains when it comes to beautiful women." She's staring at him, and he's holding her gaze.

I sit up a little straighter at her compliment, even if it's drowning in insults.

We suffer through a few more questions before Madeline is called into an important meeting. She gives Dru a hug and shakes my hand before she leaves. I'm confused. She was warm and hugged me earlier. Now she's being cold.

"You did great," Dru reassures me after she disappears on the elevator.

"Did I? Because she seemed to like me when she first met me, then she stopped." I don't know how this meeting went.

"She's weird with everyone. Sometimes she gets laser focused on something that has nothing to do with us, and we lose her attention completely. She knows she does it, and it's part of why she wants to retire. She's tired of having to split her time between family and business."

"So she doesn't hate me?" I ask, feeling only a little relief.

"No, she doesn't hate you. Who could hate you?" Dru asks before placing a kiss on my cheek. "Let's get out of here."

"Let's!" I exhale.

In the elevator, I get an email invitation from Yanique. Her engagement party is next week. I show it to Dru without saying a word.

He leans in to read the invitation, then takes my phone and starts clicking.

"What are you doing?" I reach for my phone, but he holds it out of my reach.

"I'm RSVPing with a plus one." He shows me the phone.

"So we have to do this all again next week with my family? I don't know if I can," I whine.

Dru takes both of my hands and wraps them around his waist. Then he wraps his hands around me, resting his chin on top of my head.

"You can do anything. You've never introduced a boyfriend to your parents before?" he asks as he twirls one of my curls around his finger.

"I have." I pout. "You know why it's weird this time."

He nuzzles against my hair. "No, I don't."

I pull back from our embrace and glare at him. He laughs and pulls me back in. The elevator comes to a stop on the eighth floor, and Madeline stands in front of us with a smug look on her face.

"I pressed the wrong button. I'm going up," she says, grinning as the doors close in her face.

"This is all very weird," I say into Dru's collarbone.

"That it is."

Chapter 13

Dru

For the past week, Charisse has been stressing about this engagement party we're going to today. We passed the Madeline Martin test last week, so I know we can handle anything that's thrown our way.

"Dru, you don't understand. My parents can see right through anything I try to pull. I don't know how, but I've never been able to get anything past them my whole life. Meanwhile, they kept my sister's real dad a secret from me all this time," she whines and leans against the window of the car we're riding in.

She won't be getting over that anytime soon. I understand. I hope she can accept it for what it is and move on.

"Just be yourself. Be whoever you usually are with them, and they won't suspect a thing." I pat her knee.

Chance opens my door when we reach the venue. I step out of the car and take in my surroundings before reaching in and taking Charisse's hand. Her smooth brown legs ease out of the car, and my breath hitches. She's so damn fine.

"This is nice," she says once she is completely out.

"It's nice enough. Our venue will run laps around this one." I nudge her with my elbow. She squeezes my hand and leads us in.

Before we can even get all the way into the building, we are approached by someone.

"Charisse Renea Turner, who is this?" An older woman exclaims as she squeezes my bicep and gives me a once over.

"Mom, this is my boyfriend Dru. Can you stop touching all over him please?" Charisse brushes her mother's hand off me.

I extend my hand to shake hers. She shoos it away and reaches between Charisse and me and gives me a hug. Her hands roam all over my back, and it takes some effort to shimmy out of her clutches.

"It's nice to meet you Mrs.—"

"Call me Mama Den." She steps back and gives me another once over, then juts her bottom lip out in what I can only interpret as approval. "Okay, Charisse. Okay," she says as she walks away.

"That was weirder than when you met my mom," I tease.

Charisse's face is contorted in horror and disgust. "I'm sorry. This was a terrible idea. We should just leave now." She pulls on my hand to lead me out.

"Oh no, you look too damn good in that dress to waste it. We're going to enjoy this party and conspire on how we can make ours a thousand times better," I tell her as I run a finger along her jawline and place a kiss on her cheek.

She leans into me. The tension in her body melts away. My hand slides down her back and hooks around her waist.

"Come on," I tell her and lead her toward the music pounding our ears. Tables with floral centerpieces fill half of the space. Most of the tables are full of people sitting around. The dance floor in front of the room is empty, and the impulsive part of me pulls Charisse to the vacant space...someone's got to get the dancing started.

"What are you doing?" Charisse squeals and pushes back from me the closer we get to the hardwood dance floor.

"I'm asking you for a dance." I bow in front of her and offer my hand.

She stares at my palm for an embarrassing amount of time. "You're making me look bad," I say through gritted teeth.

She shakes out of her stupor and takes my hand.

"You can dance, right?" We've never discussed dancing. I assume we can all dance, but I've met some people who prove that stereotype so terribly wrong.

"Yes, I can dance." She hisses.

"Looks like we have another set of lovebirds in the building!" the DJ announces. "Let's slow it down for them."

My absolutely favorite slow jam comes on. I turn to the DJ and give him a heads up. I'd ask how he knew, but this song is universal. I'm already swaying to the melody when I put my hand on Charisse's waist and lessen the space between us. She gasps when our bodies touch. I hold her other hand in mine, and we let the music move us while the world disappears.

Neither of us says a word, but we move in synchrony, our bodies becoming one. Charisse's tension is completely gone, and I feel at home. The song ends before either of us is ready, and a bumping and grinding song plays next. I want to see what she's got, but this is a family affair, and I don't need them seeing that right now.

"That was a terrible segue," she complains as we exit the dance floor. Mission accomplished though because about ten people are now dancing— bumping and grinding like I want to be with Charisse.

"Who is this?" a bubbly, dark-skinned beauty asks Charisse.

"Yanique, this is my boyfriend Dru. Dru, this is my sister Yanique." Charisse's tension has returned. I don't have to touch her to notice how her whole demeanor has changed.

"This is a beautiful venue, Yanique. Thanks for having us," I offer.

"How'd you meet him?" Yanique interrogates Charisse with a tone I don't like. My instinct to step in and take charge of this situation is tamped down. I'm not getting in the middle of sister shit. Charisse is on her own.

"At Lily's paint and sip a few months back." Charisse says her rehearsed lines flawlessly.

"Oh wow, something good can come from those little things, huh?" Yanique says, laughing at herself.

Charisse starts trembling, so I stand behind her and wrap my arms around her, resting my chin on her collarbone. "Risse, do you know if Lily is looking for investors? I know some people who'd be interested. She's the reason we're together."

"I'm not sure, bae. She wants to keep it small and intimate. She's living her dreams with her day job and her night job. But I'll ask. I won't assume I know and take anything out of her pockets." She angles her head to look at me, and her eyes shine when they meet mine.

"You're an investor?" Yanique asks me with a squeak in her voice.

"If I find a business worth investing in, sure. But I have some associates looking to invest in small Black-owned businesses, and Lily's is perfect." That's partially true. I'm sure I could find an investor for Lily if she really wanted one though.

"I've been looking for an investor for my event planning business Aesthetic Affairs. I put this all together myself." She waves her hand to present the space to us.

"This looks great!" Charisse says. "Dru, I'm hungry. Let's go get some food." She faces her sister. "Congrats again, Yanique. I'm so happy for you!"

I take her outstretched hand, and we walk toward the refreshments table.

"Was she really trying to get you to invest in her company?" Charisse asks, giggling.

"I think she was about to. Thank you for saving me." I give her hand a squeeze.

"This is just too much. I don't know why it's like this whenever I'm around my family, but my mom and sister rub me the wrong way constantly." She leans into me, and I rub her back.

"You can escape to the bathroom for a little break. I'll get us a table and some food," I tell her. Leaving right now will look awful. I know that's what she wants, but it'll isolate her even more. I'll be her buffer.

She nods and heads off to the bathroom. I stand and watch her walk away, admiring that sexy dress she has on. It's not overly revealing, but the way the material falls on her body fills me with heat.

I head to the bar and order drinks. I turn around and lean against the bar, surveying the place. Yanique did a great job with the space. The music is nice, and everything looks great. An investor could help take her to the next level. I wonder if that could help bridge the gap between her and Charisse.

The bartender taps on the bar to get my attention and hands me my drink. I thank him and leave a tip on the counter before I take a sip.

"What are you drinking, Dru?"

Yanique and a man who looks vaguely familiar stand in front of me. "The night's signature drink, I think. "

"Love Potion #9!" Yanique squeals. "I came up with that myself. Isn't it delicious?"
I take another swig for show and nod my head. "It's great. You're good at this!"

"Thank you!" She smiles sheepishly. "Oh, I came over here to introduce you to my fiancé Byron Jeffries. Byron, this is Dru...I didn't get your last name."

"Martin. Dru Martin," I help her out and extend my hand to shake Byron's as if this is my first meeting with him. Hearing his name triggers my memory. Byron's dating Fresh Flavor Fix's CFO, Alishia. Dating, as in, he picked her up from work two days ago and swept her away on a weekend trip.

I meet his eyes as we shake hands, and there's no pleading or guilt there. He's a stand-up fiancé and not a cheating dog.

This is not the time or place for me to say anything, but I'm telling Charisse as soon as we leave.

"Nice to meet you," I mumble, scanning the room for Charisse to get me out of this situation. I spot her coming out of the bathroom, and I sigh in relief.

"My girl is out of the bathroom. Congratulations on your engagement," I tell them and quickly make my escape.

Charisse doesn't look any better than she did when she went into the bathroom. Anxiety is etched across her face, and her body is tense. I won't be telling her what I know about her sister's fiancé just yet. Instead, I go to her and lead her to a small sitting area just outside of the main ballroom.

"What's got you?" I ask, holding her hands in mine.

"It's just awkward," she tells me, staring at the floor. "Being around them is so difficult for me. Knowing that they've held this secret from me for so long just makes me an outsider who doesn't belong in this family, which means I don't belong here right now."

I don't have words to help her, so I just hold her hand and continue to hold space for her. We sit there for about five minutes before an older gentleman walks up.

"What's the matter with my girl?" the man asks.

Charisse looks up, her face brightens for a moment, then sadness washes over her again. "Hi Daddy," she tells him, looking down again.

"Who did what to you, girl?" he asks, coming in closer. I have no idea what to do. She needs comfort, but she's not making any move toward her father, and I don't want to leave her on her own right now if that's not what she wants. So I wait quietly.

"Nobody did anything to me Daddy." She sighs, and I can see that she's weighing her options and wondering if she should bring this up now or just let it go. She's having a hard time letting it go, but again I follow her lead, and I just keep holding her hand.

"Will you dance with me?" her father asks, kneeling to be face-to-face with her.

I feel her body relax a little, and a smile stretches across her face.

"I'd love to dance with you Daddy," she says. I give her hand a squeeze and sit back on the bench while she goes and dances with her father. Maybe they'll talk it out while they dance. Or maybe she'll just enjoy the moment and get to everything else later on.

I want to hide because this is a very overwhelming situation. This isn't the typical way to meet family for the first time, so I didn't imagine it being like this. I'm ready for this evening to end.

I'm sitting, scrolling through my socials and reminding myself to take a picture of us to post when Byron slithers into the seat next to me. I roll my eyes and don't let him hear the deep breath that I take. I don't want to deal with this shit right now. I don't want to deal with this shit ever if I'm being honest, but he's bringing it right to me at his own engagement party.

"Hey man, you did me a solid up there earlier," Byron tells me, reaching out his hand to dap me up.

I don't take his hand. I don't want to touch him or be near him or hear any of his lies. I want no parts of this charade at all. I can't even imagine how much work her sister put into this for her cheating fiancé. What's the endgame is the question I do want to ask him. It's insane to think that he might just do this during their whole marriage. Why did he even propose?

"Why are you marrying her?" I blurt out before I can stop myself. Shit, I said I wasn't getting involved.

"Cuz that's what she wants. She's been pressuring me to settle down since the day we met, and I'm just going to give her what she wants," he answers with this shrug.

"And you'll take what you want on the side?" I ask. This man has no moral code, no sense of right and wrong. I don't even want to be sitting here with him anymore.

"We'll see, but I appreciate your silence. And I'd appreciate your continued silence." He gets up and walks away before I can answer.

Now I'm really ready to leave; everything about this party feels wrong. Maybe that's what Charisse is feeling and not the anxiety about her family. She senses the wrongness of this whole situation.

She doesn't look great over there dancing with her father. They're not talking or smiling. So, I take it upon myself to get us out of here.

I lean forward and hold my stomach and walk slowly toward her. She spots me immediately and rushes toward me.

"Oh my God! What's wrong?" she asks, her hand on my back.

"I'm ready to get the fuck out of here." I whisper to her as she puts her arm around me and helps me stand upright.

"You're faking?" she whispers.

"Yes. let's go."

"If I wasn't fake marrying you, I'd actually marry you for this right here." She tells me as we make our way to the door. Right outside the door, I text Chance that we are ready to go. It takes less than two minutes for him to pull up to the doors and pick us up.

"What made you go through such drastic measures?" She asks me once we're in the back of the car.

"I don't know if you want to know, but you hate secrets, so I'm going to tell you. It's bad."

The color drains from her face, and I can see the tension in her body return yet again.

"The quick and dirty of it is that your sister's fiancé is cheating on her." There's no way to mince words. She leans back in her seat and crosses her arms over her chest.

"Really?" It's not an accusatory question by any means. I can tell she believes me, but she's just in disbelief.

"Yeah. he's been dating my CFO for a few months now." I pull up Alishia's socials and show Charisse the pictures of them together on the vacation they took last weekend.

She clutches my phone and scrolls through the pictures more. "These get more scandalous as you go. I can't believe this. Yanique is going to be crushed." She hands my phone back to me and starts rubbing her temples.

"I know, but this wasn't the place to say a word about it." I don't know anything about her sister or their relationship other than that it's strained, but I didn't want any part in deceiving a woman like this. It feels gross right now to still be holding the secret from her while she's celebrating their engagement.

"What do I do?" Charisse asks.

"That's not for me to decide. You might need to call your girls for this one. My instinct was to punch him in the face." I confess. She bursts into laughter, and it's a sweet sound after such a tumultuous evening with her family.

"I love that sound," I tell her. I can't control my hand as it stretches out to caress her face. She's beautiful.

At my touch, her laughter dies down. She looks into my eyes, and I can't help myself. I lean forward and place my lips on hers. It's a soft gentle kiss at first, but she doesn't pull away, so neither do I. Her lips are soft as I thought they would be. And the sound that comes out of her is like no other sound I've ever heard. It ignites me, and the kiss becomes fervent. I slide my hand from her face to the back of her neck and pull her closer to me. Her lips part, and I take that as an invitation, sliding my tongue in and caressing hers. She moans into my mouth, and I lose my composure for a moment, using my other hand to pull her onto my lap and press her body against mine. She moves willingly and straddles me, then plunges her tongue into my mouth. I savor her taste and the feel of her body.

"Boss, we're here," Chance says through the intercom.

Charisse slides off me and wipes at the corner of her mouth. I want to go in her apartment, but I don't want to pressure her. And I don't know what state she's in after everything with her family today. So I step out of the car, and I walk her to her door.

"Today was—" I start, but I can't finish my sentence because she's on me again, kissing me and wrapping her arms around me.

"Come inside with me," she whispers after she breaks our kiss and holds my hand while opening her door.

"Are you sure?" I ask her. This is going to complicate our arrangement.

"This can be our cheat meal. We give in just once, and then we forget about it." She says as she stands there, looking like she might not survive another minute without me. She's in a bad spot, and she needs to process everything that went down today. I don't want her to hate herself in the morning for being impulsive.

"I-I can't. I won't. Tonight was rough for you, and I'm not going to be your distraction tonight. You need to deal with how you're feeling." I place a peck on her check and let her hand go.

"I'll call you tomorrow," I tell her before I walk out of her apartment.

Chapter 14

Charisse

Shortly after I step out of the shower, feeling gross for what I tried to do with Dru, I hear a knock at my door. God, I hope it's not Dru. I can't face him right now or maybe ever again. My face heats up just thinking about it.

"Who is it?" I ask, wrapping my towel tighter around me and padding to the door to look out the peephole.

"It's us," a familiar voice calls out.

My girls are here. I wrench the door open, and they pile in, arms full of bags.

"We brought some feelings for you to eat," Lily calls out, holding up her bag.

"How'd you know I needed you?" I sigh.

"Your boyfriend called us and sent Chance to pick us up. Go put on some sweats, so we can be comfy and sad," Porsche tells me.

I obey. Dressed in my softest sweats, I return to my living room and find a buffet of junk.

"You know the way to my heart." I sigh. The brownies look

divine. I snag one and bite into it, and all my worries melt away.

"Tell us everything," Lily says while she munches on some chips.

I look from Porsche to Lily, and they're both staring, waiting for me to spill.

I tell them everything, and their mouths hang open when I'm finished.

"So, Mama Den felt him up, your sister tried to get him to be her investor, and he knows her fiancé is a cheating asshole?" Porsche summarizes everything.

"Yep, that's the rundown of the engagement party. There's more though." My stomach clenches as I recall how I basically mounted him in the car, and how he shut me down after starting it all.

"We kissed," I confess, suddenly finding my brownie very interesting.

"Really?" Porsche draws out. "Was it good?" A devilish look is on her face.

"Be serious, Porsche!" Lily scolds, frowning at her.

"That's not all," I say, hanging my head even lower.

"Bitch, did y'all fuck?!" Porsche practically screams as she jumps out of her seat.

Lily glares at Porsche, but she doesn't say a word. She wants to know too.

"I tried to. He turned me down." I finally look up at them, having confessed all my shame.

"So the kiss had to be good if you tried to get him into your bed," Porsche deduces. She's calculating something.

I shake my head at her, still too embarrassed to laugh.

"Why'd he turn you down? Was he trying to stick to the agreement?" Porsche continues her questioning.

"No," Lily butts in. "She's a mess today, and he didn't want to take advantage of her." She side-eyes Porsche. Finally, I let my laugh tumble out.

"He gave me a valiant speech about exactly that. It didn't take the sting of rejection away though." I wouldn't have regretted it, not with how good I imagine he is.

I sigh, and Porsche cuts her eyes at me. "You really just want him, don't you?"

I shrug, trying to play it off. "Physically, yeah. Who wouldn't?"

"You're right cuz I'd fuck him on your kitchen counter with you in the other room if he was down for it." A wave of nausea comes over me at the image she just painted.

"Not just physically," Lily says, looking at me with knowing eyes. "You're falling for him, and you're about to be in deep shit."

"No I'm—"

"Bitch, yes you are! I can see it in your eyes. You say his name all slow. You like the way it feels in your mouth...and want to feel something else in your mouth. I know you." Porsche points at me and grins.

"Shut up!" is all I can say. She's not wrong, but I'm not one hundred percent ready to admit that.

"I told you this would happen. How do you spend all that time with someone, getting to know them and all of that and not develop any feelings? He's gorgeous. He's the perfect guy for you: money or no money."

"But he has the money," Porsche adds. "Lots of it!"

I don't respond. There's nothing I can say. Both of them are right. Of course, I'd meet the perfect guy and have some stupid arrangement that keeps us from really being together.

"Are you two staying the night?" I ask, faking a yawn and stretching my arms. I need some space, but I don't want to put them out.

"No, Chance said we should text him when we're ready to go, and he'd be back to get us," Lily says as she pulls out her phone.

"Thanks for coming over. You helped me feel a little better," I lie. They made me feel worse with this new realization. "I'm tired though, and I'm going to hit the sack."

Each of them gives me a hug, and I walk to my room and lay across the bed, scrolling socials on my phone. I check out Dru's profile, and seeing him makes my heart squeeze. He's beautiful.

His latest post is about me, and it sounds so sweet and genuine. He might really mean it and isn't just doing it for the views he's trying to get. All of the comments say that I'm a keeper, or they think he's finally found the one. I smile, happy that his plan is working. Our engagement won't come as a surprise to anyone. But another part of me is gutted by the fact that this is all a farce. It's a financial arrangement and not the real relationship it's starting to feel like.

When my phone buzzes in my hand, I know it's him before I lay my eyes on his name popping up on the screen. I take a deep breath before answering.

"Hey Dru!" I say, trying to sound as peppy and bright as I can.

"Do you feel better after talking to your girls?" he asks, concern flecked in his voice.

"A little. Thanks for sending them. It was very thoughtful of you." I smile. He's been thoughtful with me from the moment we met. I never knew that was such an endearing quality someone could have.

"You needed someone, and you and I would have gotten tangled together if I'd tried to help." He chuckles, and the sound of it makes me ache.

Would that be so bad? Us tangled together would make me feel immensely better.

"Yeah." I sigh.

"What?"

I sigh again. "Nothing. At least nothing that can be fixed, I guess," I say, hoping he thinks I'm still upset about my family drama. I am a little, but it's him that has me in knots right now.

"Well, I'm beat, so I'm going to get some sleep. Have a good night Dru," I whisper.

"Have a good night, Charisse."

Chapter 15

Dru

I don't like the sound of her voice. It's missing her usual chipperness. I know she had a rough day, but she sounds more off than I'm okay with. I pace around my living room after we get off the phone, feeling unsure about my next move.

"You good, chief?" Hunter asks when he answers the phone.

"Nothing's seriously wrong, but I'm struggling," I say to him, hesitant about how much I should share with him. He's my lawyer and has always been discreet with my personal matters, but this is different.

"I knew this was going to happen," he says, and I can hear the laugh he's stifling, but I don't know what he's talking about.

"Knew what?"

"I'm going to be real with you, okay? I've seen your socials. I read that post you made today. You don't write like that over a business transaction. You meant that shit. And you are all googly-eyed in your pictures together. You can cut the shit with me. I knew from the moment I saw her." He huffs and laughs out loud this time.

"You knew what exactly?" He's treading into dangerous waters here, and I don't like it.

"You want me to say it so you don't have to?" he asks, still laughing.

No, I don't want him to say it because then I'll have to face it, and that will fuck everything up.

"Nah man, keep that locked up."

"You got it," he says. "For what it's worth, you look genuinely happy for the first time in a long time."

"Alright man, I'm going to let you go. Sorry for bothering you."

"I'll add this to your billable hours," he says with a laugh and hangs up.

I'm not falling for her. I care about her, yes, but falling for her is a whole different monster. I just don't want to see her hurting, and the way she looked when I left was heartbreaking. She looked destroyed.

I need to know if she's all right. I won't be able to sleep tonight without knowing. I grab my keys and head to the elevator.

Regret pulsates through my body as I stand at her door with my hand raised to knock on it. What am I doing here?

I lower my hand and turn to walk away, but she's right in there, and I want to see her. Fuck.

Hunter's right.

I knock on her door, and I wait with my heart pounding out my chest. I close my eyes and take a few deep breaths, praying she doesn't answer until I've gotten myself together.

"Dru?" I hear her say through the door. The sounds of the door unlocking loosens me up. This is Charisse, and we are friends, and I can come and check on her without taking things to another level.

"What are you doing here? Is everything okay? Where's Chance? Is he okay?" Her eyes are darting all over the parking lot.

"Chance is fine. He's off right now. I gotta let that man live his life sometimes. I didn't like how I left you, so I came back to check on you."

She averts her eyes and steps aside to let me in.

"Don't make this weird, Charisse," I say, pulling her into a hug. She smells like coconut oil and vanilla. I breathe in her scent and forget what I came here for.

"I'm trying not to. I tried to seduce you earlier. And if that's not embarrassing enough, you rejected me." She buries her head in my chest, and I pray that she can't feel my heart thundering.

I didn't want to turn her down. It took every last ounce of my self-control to walk away. It's taking all of my control now not to kiss her. She doesn't really want me though. She really was just trying to be distracted. I'm not breaking that boundary again.

"I shouldn't have kissed you in the car. It was an unscheduled kiss, and I'm sorry," I tell her, putting my hands in the pockets of my gray sweatpants.

"I straddled you, Dru. I didn't not want it." She stares into my eyes, and I almost crumble.

"Oh yeah?" is all I can muster up.

"My friends think I'm falling in love with you," she confesses, sheepishly meeting my eyes.

"Is that so?" I hang on every moment until she speaks again.

"Yes, they do."

"What do you think?" I ask her, treading dangerous territory.

She considers before answering, biting her bottom lip and looking away from me.

"I think they might be right," she says, looking up at me.

Shit. My throat suddenly goes dry, and I feel like I can't take a breath in. I cough awkwardly for far too long. Charisse disentangles herself from me to grab a glass of water. I continue to cough as she hands it to me. I suck in a deep breath and put the glass to my lips.

I don't know what to do. My mind and body have both shut down all non-essential operations. If I stay here any longer, I'm going to combust right in front of her. I need to get the hell out of here and figure this shit out.

"I have to leave," I say, not daring to look at her as I make a beeline for her front door. She's going to hate me for making two hasty exits today, but I can't process all of this right here, right now. I need to go.

I slip out of her apartment and practically sprint to my car. I brave a glance at her door, and she's standing there, watching me, looking even sadder than when I left earlier today. I can't. We can't. This isn't a part of the plan. It's not in our contract. There's no caveat or addendum to falling in love with each other.

I drive straight to my studio. My mind needs something to concentrate on, and my hands need something to do. Once I'm inside, I sit down at my desk and sketch. The design comes to me effortlessly. It's going to be a beautiful piece. I figure out the dimensions, and gather up the supplies. I'll stay here all night to finish this if I have to.

The measuring and cutting and sanding give me so much clarity. I need to stay the course with Charisse. I wasn't trying to really find a wife. Finding Charisse was dumb luck: being in the right place at the right time—twice. And this is nothing more than a business arrangement. Of course, we'll think we're falling for one another after all the time we've spent together. We're both great people. Who's not drawn to someone great?

I have no idea what time it is as I stain the piece I just made. It's probably one of my best pieces ever. As the first coat dries, I stand back and really check out my work. It's remarkable. And as I inspect it, I realize it's the coffee table to match the end table Charisse loved so much.

Shit.

Chapter 16

Charisse

After a couple of bottles of wine, I slept like a baby last night. It took that much alcohol to calm the rage inside of me. That man led me on and rejected me twice in one night. The second time hurt more than the first. I don't want to see him at all today. I don't want to see him anymore, but I'm under contract. I can't believe he did that to me. I understood the first time, but I thought he came back to finish what he started. Instead, he let me be completely vulnerable, then he ran away.

I'm canceling all of my feelings for him. They've expired. They're dead. They never existed in the first place.

My phone dings. It's my reminder to pay my bills today and update my budget. I sigh, knowing I'm about to be pissed off all over again when I log into my bank account and see that I have just enough to cover this month's bills and no money for anything else. I'll have to be resourceful with my meals. Dru has helped out a lot with that over these past few weeks, and I do have money left over from what he sent me to go dress shopping with. I perk up. I might be good this month.

I use my thumb to log into my banking app, and something's wrong. I log out and log back in, but it doesn't change. There's $250,000 in my account. My hands start to tremble. I log out and back in a few more times. Then I use the internet browser to log in. The number stays the same the whole time. Tears spring to my eyes at this windfall until I realize where it came from.

"Lily, I bared my soul to his ass last night. I told him I was falling for him, and he left in a flash, and I wake up this morning to a quarter of a million dollars." It's hard to even say that out loud. "He paid me off to remind me that I'm just business to him. I'm just a transaction. All of our interactions have been billable, and he's paying his debt."

Lily's face on the screen of my phone is thoughtful, with a touch of sympathy. She's not making a judgment just yet.

"I don't know what to tell you," she says, twisting her mouth to the side. "I knew you'd catch feelings. How could you not? What do you want to do moving forward?"

"I want to go slash his tires, but I'm sure he can get them fixed instantly. I want to break up with him, but we aren't even dating."

"You want him to feel the hurt you're feeling right now?" Lily surmises.

I nod. "Exactly."

"What do you think he's feeling right now?" she asks with warmth in her eyes.

"I don't care." I pout.

"Yes you do. You're falling for him, and you do care. You just don't want to admit it. So stop and think about what he's feeling right now."

I scowl at her. "Whose side are you on?"

"I'm on your side, but sometimes you aren't even on your own side. I'm looking out for you. You called me instead of Porsche for a reason, and you know it."

She's right. Porsche was going to try to get me to go shopping and to just revel in the money and keep playing the game, feelings be damned. I don't want to do that. I can't do that.

"Do you think he's wrestling with his feelings for me?" I ask Lily, but I already know the answer. He is, of course. Why else would he run?

Lily gives me a knowing look, and I laugh. She's the wisdom of our trio. This is why I called her.

"So, what are you going to do?" she asks.

"I'm going to give him space and let him come to me. I'm going to let my feelings simmer and let him take the lead. And I'm going to keep my part of the contract." What else can I do?
"How do you feel about that?" Lily asks, ever the life coach.

"I don't feel as terrible as I did earlier, but I'm still not happy." I bite my lip.

"I'll accept that."

We say our goodbyes, and I log into my bank account again. I want to take a screenshot, but the app won't let me.

"You need to pay these damn bills," I tell myself. I can pay off all of my debt right now and still have more than half of the money. "Fuck it!" I say as I log in to my student loan account and click "Current Balance." I breathe in slowly through my nose and then I click the "Pay Now" button.

Then I move on to my car and do the same thing, having a hard time believing this is my life. I pay off every debt I have, and for the first time in my life, I open up a savings account. I'm sure there are better ways to store your money, but all I know right now are the basics: checking account and savings account. Now I have one of both.

Dru texts me later on in the day.

Dru: Did you get your first payment?

I laugh, not at all surprised that he's glossing over everything that happened last night.

Me: Yes, much to my surprise. It was awkward getting it after what happened last night. It made me feel kind of gross.

If he won't bring it up, I will. I have time to grade three whole essays before I get a response from him.

Dru: Shit. I can see that. I'm sorry. It was in my calendar to do it today, so I did.

Me: Can we talk about what happened last night?

There's another long pause before he answers.

Dru: I don't want to complicate things. We have everyone convinced, and if we add real feelings to it, this will get muddled. I'm just thinking about my endgame here.

I hate what he's saying, but he's got a point. We started this for a reason, and if we give in to feelings now, that reason is compromised.

Me: I hate that you're right.

Dru: Are you busy next weekend?

Me: That's a horrible segue. But of course I'm not.

Dru: Good, my mother's annual charity ball is next Saturday night. Will you be my contractually obligated date?

I send him a GIF to show how disgusted I am with his phrasing. He sends me back one of someone falling off a chair laughing.

Me: Yes, I will be your date to your mother's charity ball. Do I have to use my own money to buy a dress?

I can sense him cracking up all the way from his penthouse

Dru: How much do you need?

Me: I need however much you think. And I need you to take me shopping. I need something spectacular. Something so insanely expensive that I feel uncomfortable wearing it.

Dru: I'll pick you up tomorrow at 8am. Have a good day, Charisse.

Well, that's going to give me anxiety all day today. I love and hate surprises. They're usually wonderful, but the anxiety leading up to them, whether it's an hour of waiting or twenty-four of them, drives me crazy.

I'll do my job and grade the never-ending pile of essays in my bag. I promised to have these done by Monday, and I've done nothing but hurt my own feelings all weekend long.

I spend the day grading. I actually fall asleep on the couch with essays in my hand, and I'm awakened by the sound of knocking on my door.

I jolt up and grab my phone. It's eight in the morning. Shit! I was supposed to be ready.

Dru laughs at me when I open the door with wild eyes and still in yesterday's clothes. "I knew I should have called when I was on my way."

"Give me fifteen minutes," I tell him, then I jet away into my bathroom to shower. Behind the closed door, I do some deep breathing to calm myself down. My feelings for him haven't been canceled. They're on front street. They're prominent and unyielding.

I rush through my shower, and when I step out and see my hair, my stomach clenches. Back to the shower I go to drench my hair and get these curls to act right. I know I don't have time to diffuse it, so I pull it into a ponytail and hope for the best.

It's 8:12 when I emerge from my room in some loose fitting jeans and a crop top. Dru's eyes are on my waist, and I smile. My new life goal will be to drive him crazy. It's working so far.

"Ready!"

He grabs my keys from the counter and holds them out for me. With my purse and phone in hand, I slide past him and out the door. Chance waits for me with the car door open and a bright smile on his face.

"Good morning, Chance! How are you doing today?" I ask him, taking his outstretched hand and stepping into the car.

"I'm doing well, Miss Charisse. You look nice today," he tells me as he closes my door. Dru gets in the car. He's on his phone texting.

"The airport," he tells Chance before pressing the button to bring the partition up in the car.

"Are you about to ladynap me and sell my parts on the black market?" I ask him.

He laughs, loudly. "You're ridiculous. No. I'm taking you to get a dress for the charity ball."

"We can't go to the mall?" I ask.

"You want a mall dress to go to a charity ball run by a billionaire?" He raises his eyebrows.

"No, I'd feel like the pauper that I am. I do need something to help me look the part."

His expression changes for just a moment, then he's smiling at me again.

"Where are we going then?" I ask. I have no idea where he could be taking me.

"New York. My favorite designer is waiting for us."

"Your who is what?" I ask. I'm having a hard time breathing. This isn't my life.

He laughs at me and pats my hand.

"Do I have my ID?" I say out loud, rummaging through my purse. Sometimes I leave my wallet in my car. I didn't even think about it. "We can't go if I don't have my ID. Let me find my wallet. If we have to turn back, will we miss our flight?" It's just my luck I'm getting swept away, and I didn't have the forethought to take all my necessary items. I'm about to dump my purse all the way out when Dru puts his hands on mine.

"We can't be late. And you'll be fine if you don't have your ID. We're taking the family plane. Just relax."

The family what? I understand family homes and family traditions. I don't understand the concept of a family plane. I find my wallet and sit back in my chair, content. I have to stop being surprised by the rich people shit they do. They are rich people. Even with six digits in my account right now, I'm poor.

We drive on to the runway and walk right into the plane. I push down the urge to send a group text to my friends. This is everyday life for Dru. I need to learn to fit in...or at least not stick out so much.

"Do you already have a dress in mind for me?" I ask Dru once we've settled into our seats. The plane is taxiing and getting ready to take off.

"I have several. They're one of a kind pieces. I won't tell you which is my favorite, but you can really pick anything in the store." He drains the drink the single flight attendant gave him when he boarded. He has a routine for when he gets on board, and this lady knows it well.

My excitement builds thinking about trying on these dresses and being able to pick just one. I'm also excited to spend the day with Dru. I grin at him.

"What?"

"This is an unscheduled outing. Am I breaking you?" I say, chuckling.

"Maybe this is who I am underneath my mask. Maybe you're seeing the real me." He winks at me, and I melt a little.

"Just wait until you finally meet the real me then," I shoot back.

I hope that happens sooner than later. I'm starting to feel more and more comfortable with him, but after yesterday, some of my walls went back up.

Chapter 17

Charisse

I look spectacular in this dress. Dru can't take his eyes off me. I chose his favorite one. And I know I look delicious in it. The room goes dead silent when we walk in, and I want to believe it's because of me.

"Charisse, tell me that's a custom Isolde Orion. He had it made for you. You're absolutely beautiful in that dress," Dru's mother tells me as she gives me a hug. "He's so taken by you," she whispers in my ear and squeezes my shoulders. My heart drops. She really seems to like me. Lying to her feels terrible.

I force a smile on my face. "Thank you. I feel beautiful."

"You two have fun," she tells us before she goes back into the party and mingles with her guests.

A waiter holds a platter of champagne flutes. Dru picks up two. He looks anxious, and he quickly downs one. I hold my hand out to take the other, and he downs that one too. I didn't think he'd get weird around his family.

Draymond approaches us, a cheshire grin on his face. "You two have to be serious for you to bring her to this," he says to Dru, jabbing him in his rib. He takes my right hand and brings it to his lips. I cover my mouth to hide the girlish smile I can't stop from appearing.

Dru slaps his brother's hand off mine and holds it. "Stop that, weirdo. A simple hello will suffice."

Draymond's laughter echoes through the ballroom. "He's super serious about you. What did you do to him?" he asks me before he takes a dramatic step backward and bows. His brother is a fool, and I love it.

Draymond's twin Drummond sneaks up behind him and grabs his ass. Draymond doesn't even jump.

"Can you two have some decorum for once?" Dru asks, irritation showing on his face.

"She hasn't taken that stick out of his ass," Drummond says while he leans against Draymond's shoulder.

"Ass play comes later," I say before I can stop myself.

"Ooooh damn!" the twins yell in sync, covering their mouths with opposite hands but in the exact same way.

My heart melts completely. They're so dang cute.

I don't dare to look at Dru. I know what face he's making, and I can hear his voice asking me why I had to say that.

"I like this one, Dru," Drummond says. He reaches out to shake my hand, but Draymond gives him a look, and Drummond backs away and bows.

I can't. I burst into laughter. They're both fools. A double dose of foolery and shenanigans. I want to hang out with them sometime.

"I love them!" I tell Dru. He just rolls his eyes and takes my hand, leading me deeper into the crowd. He's off today.

I pull back from him and lean in close to him. "Are you okay today?" I whisper in his ear. He smells divine, and I linger to breathe him in more.

"I'm fine. My brothers are children, and it gets on my nerves. They can't act right no matter the situation," he mutters, frowning.

"Why are you letting it bother you? How old are they?"

"They're thirty-one. They always get drunk at this ball. They're going to go too far with it."

"Says the man who chugged two flutes of champagne without taking a single breath," I tease.

He doesn't smile at me.

Music starts playing. "Let's dance!" I urge him. He grumbles but follows me to the dance floor filled with people. The crowd is much more hype than at my sister's engagement party.

The typical line dance song plays, and I fall in line, kicking and hopping and dropping it as the instructions tell me to. Dru's dancing too, but he's going through the motions. I almost see him saying each step of the dance in his head. I watch him, and he looks absolutely miserable. I hop in front of him, pulling his hands onto my waist, and we follow the dance moves together. He's tense at first, a bag of sticks, but after three rounds, he loosens up and moves with rhythm.

I twirl around and face him, holding his hands as we move together. His face brightens. He's having fun, and I even see a smile looking back at me. I grin at him and move in closer so that our bodies are touching. He wraps his hands around my waist, and we kind of sway to the music as the song ends. The DJ follows up with a slow song. Dru's mouth curls into another smile, and he sighs.

"What?" I ask.

"This is my favorite song, ever."

"Oh yeah?"

"Most definitely." He tightens his hold on me and rests his chin on the top of my head. It's a simple, but intimate move. We are a lock and key.

At the end of the song, the DJ starts talking. "I believe Dru Martin has an announcement for the crowd. Untangle yourself from your beautiful date and get to it!"

Dru releases me and heads to the DJ booth without giving me a second look. He grabs the mic and takes an awkward deep breath into it. I look around the ballroom and see that his brothers and his mother are all as lost as everyone else here. Then I hear my name.

"Charisse Turner, I didn't think that when I met you while creating the ugliest painting of my life, that you'd capture my heart in such a short amount of time. But I can be myself around you. I am myself when I'm around you. Everyone in this room can see how beautiful you are on the outside, but inside, you're a rare gem. The most perfect diamond, unblemished and worth all the gold in the world. You make me feel alive. You make me feel happy. And I know I don't deserve to have someone as perfect as you, but if you'll have me, I'll spend my life working to be someone who deserves the love you so freely give to me."

He puts the mic down and makes his way back to me. The crowd parts, most of them leave the stage. Dru kneels down in front of me. I stand there, dumbfounded. I'm not smiling or laughing or crying. He genuinely surprised me with this. My brain clicks back on when he takes my hand. "Charisse Turner, will you marry me?"

Tears well up in my eyes. What he said was so sweet and so perfect for an engagement, but I think he meant it. I kneel down with him, and the crowd laughs. I take his face in my hands and nod my yes. He stands and helps me up, then he pulls me in for our scheduled kiss.

At first, when our faces are a breath apart, he stares into my eyes, and I swear I see a flicker in them. I can't convince myself that his feelings match mine, but he's not void of feelings for me.

He runs his hand along my cheek and jaw until it's holding my chin, then he leans forward just enough for our lips to touch. It's soft and gentle, full of restraint. He pulls back, but this needs to be more convincing than that. I wrap my arms around his neck and turn my head slightly. He presses his lips on mine again, and this time I open my mouth, offering him entrance. He hesitates, so I moan in his mouth. His fingers twitch where they rest on my waist, and his tongue finds its way between my lips. He tastes like champagne.

I move my hands up his neck and caress the back of his head. He growls, and I press myself harder against him. The crowd's cheering and clapping. I don't want to pull away, but we can't stand here and kiss all night. I hug him and whisper in his ear. "You got me so good!"

He grins at me and holds my hand as we leave the now empty dance floor and go greet all the people who want to congratulate us.

We smile and accept the congratulations from three people.

"Do you know all of these people?" I ask him.

"Yes. I know them all."

"That sounds exhausting."

"There's maybe 150 people here. I know them, but I don't deal with them every day. You see that many students a day, don't you?" he asks.

"Damn, you're right." I laugh.

"Did you think about quitting when you checked your account yesterday?" he asks, grinning.

"Actually, no. It didn't cross my mind at all. I got upset. Then I paid off all of my debt and opened my first savings account." I avoid his gaze, instead focusing on the breathtaking woman coming toward us.

"You got engaged, and you haven't even introduced me to her yet?" She scolds Dru and slaps him on the shoulder.

I try to keep my features neutral and let him manage this run-in.

"Dreya, this is my fiancée Charisse. Charisse, this is my *older* sister Dreya."

"Older and better." She smiles and gives me a hug. "You sure are pretty." She turns to him. "You're right, you don't deserve her. You're a bum, but you took Mom seriously when she said you needed to settle down, didn't you?" She lightly punches his shoulder again.

"Your mom told you to settle down?" I ask, making my eyes go wide.

"No, it's not like that," Dreya says, coming to Dru's defense. "A few months ago, Mom said she wanted Dru to not focus so much on work, and he did just that because he found you."

Guilt eats at me over how genuinely happy she is for us. And for how she believes this is a real engagement, but I smile at her instead.

"Well, it's nice to meet you, future sister!" She gives me a tight squeeze and saunters off. She stops in her tracks and looks back at Dru, mouthing, "Mom's coming."

He gives her a head nod and straightens up his tie. He's nervous about his mom's reaction. I reach for his hand and smile up at him. Then I move closer to him, letting him wrap his other arm around me, so she sees us canoodling.

"Dru Landon Martin," Madeline calls out with fake venom in her voice. Her smile gives it all away. "You little sneak!" She hugs him and rocks him side to side. Her excitement is palpable. She's happy for him, for us.

"And sweet, beautiful Charisse. Welcome to the family! I can't believe that just happened!" she exclaims, clapping her hands together.

"Neither can I! He didn't give me any indication. Not even a hint." I glare at him and grin.

"He didn't send you to get your nails done?" she asks as she takes my left hand and examines the ring.

I forgot all about the ring, too busy focusing on the ruse. When I truly see it, my eyes just about pop out of my head. The rock is enormous, bigger than a digit on my finger. Where are these kinds of diamonds found? How much did this cost?

Dru leans against the wall, arms crossed over his chest while his mother and I admire his work. He's hard to read right now, but I know he's not feeling happy at the moment.

"Dru, this ring is flawless, like your future bride, right?" His mother winks at him and cups his face in her hands. "My Dru Poo is getting married!" She claps her hands and wanders off into the crowd.

Dru's face matches my feelings. He looks disgusted and guilty. We're going to have to talk about these feelings we have about lying to everyone. We hadn't factored in their joy at our union.

Chapter 18

Dru

We're quiet as we ride back to Charisse's place. She's Cinderella on her way back home from the ball, and I'm just a piece of trash who lies to everyone in his family, getting their hopes up so I can manipulate my way into the corner office of SoftScape. It's low, and it's the worst thing I've ever done.

"I hate it too," Charisse says to me as I sulk in the back of the car. She looks sick to her stomach. I am sick to my stomach.

"Can I come in so we can talk?" I ask her when we pull up to her apartment.

She glares at me, and I throw my hands up in the air. "We do need to talk. Come on."

She nods slightly and reaches for Chance's hand to slip out of the car.

She sits on her couch, and I sit in her armchair, a safe distance away. Her body language tells me she's closed off to me and anything I have to say, and honestly, I get it and I even deserve it.

I clear my throat before I speak. "I wish we'd never done this," I blurt out.

The look of hurt on her face stabs me in my heart.

"No, not because of you. Because of me. I'm conniving and weak for pulling this on my family. If I'd just asked for your number and started dating you for real, who knows where we'd be? That proposal might have been real tonight."

She scowls at me, and even bares her teeth. My words are not hitting their mark. They are slipping past the mark and splattering all over the wall instead.

I hang my head in my hands and squeeze my temples. "I just meant I did this the coward's way, and instead of genuinely searching for the woman of my dreams, I accidentally found her and locked her into a legally binding contract."

"Break the contract then. Let's just end it now," she whispers.

I can't say I haven't thought about it, but what good will that do? I'll be back at square one and Charisse won't have the money she needs. And I won't get to see her anymore.

I don't respond. That's a cop out and not a real solution. "We have to finish what we started."

"Says who?" she shoots back.

"Says me and my lawyer," I reply. I get up to leave. I shouldn't have tried to have this talk now. We are both on edge about what happened tonight. Continuing this conversation will only make it worse.

Back in the car, I know exactly where I need to go after Chance drops me off at home. The ride back to my place seems to take an hour. The privacy screen is down, and Chance keeps looking at me in the rearview mirror.

"What is it?" I mutter as we pull into the parking garage.

"Sir, I know what's going on. You have my discretion, as usual, but I thought you should know that I know." He pauses and stares at me through the mirror, waiting for me to respond. I just nod for him to continue.

"You're in love with her, and you need to just tell her. Whatever happens with your arrangement can be up to you all, but it's eating both of you up to hide your feelings. They are clear as day. Everyone believes your relationship is real because, for all intents and purposes, it is real. You have fallen for her." He finishes and looks dead in my eyes.

He's right, dammit. He's fucking right.

I don't say anything as I get out of the car except to tell him I'll have Hunter draw up an NDA for him and that he has the rest of the week off with double pay.

I walk straight to my car and drive to my workshop about five minutes away. I need to make something wild. I don't sketch or measure, I just start cutting.

Charisse thinks we should end the contract. Does that mean she wants to be done with me? She's paid off all of her debts, so she doesn't even need the rest of the money.

The curve I was supposed to be making ended up as an S shape instead. I chuck the wood to the side and grab a new piece. My head needs to be clear, but I can't stop thinking. I can't stop worrying about how royally I've screwed up my life.

Charisse is my dream woman. She compliments and completes me well. Being around her is an adventure, and it's a joy to put a smile on her face. She's a beauty, and she can hold a conversation. She's spectacular, and I've already blown it with her by being in this fake relationship.

Jumping under contract with her before spending any time together to notice the chemistry we have is my life's greatest mistake at this point.

I've screwed up the next piece of wood, and I throw it to the side too. Placing the third piece on the table, I slice it in half on the first run through the saw.

"Fuck!" I yell, throwing both pieces across the shop. "I can't even build anymore."

***

I slept terribly last night, and I'm dragging at the office today. Working in my shop tends to soothe whatever ails me emotionally, but all that happened in my shop last night was stress on top of my stress. I made a pile of garbage, which is exactly how I felt. It's a mirror to what I've done with all of this.

My acquisition still hasn't gone through. I'm hunched over my desk, stewing over the details with a fine-tooth comb when the door to my office creaks open. I leave it creaky, so I know if someone's coming. I'm in between assistants right now, and it's been working out well enough that I don't know if I really need one.

When I look up and see who it is, I realize an assistant would have fielded this disaster for me.

"You look absolutely miserable for someone who got engaged last night," her voice says, dripping with sex.

"Khalia, what are you doing here?" I ask, feeling the tension build up in my neck and shoulders.

"I'm here to tell you that you're making a mistake," she says, standing with her arms crossed over her chest.

I close my eyes and take a slow, calming breath. It has no effect on me. I still want to toss her out the window.

"Don't act like that toward me," she whines. "After all the time we spent together. After learning all of the ways we are compatible. After having all the fun we had when we were together. After all of that, Dru Martin, you should be marrying me." She finishes her little spiel and sits down in the chair across from my desk.

"What?"

"Dru, you told me you'd never said I love you to anyone before when you said it to me. Did you really say it to that teacher you got engaged to?" She scoffs. "A teacher? Really?"

My anger rises to a dangerous level, so I get up from my desk, walk to the open door, and leave her alone in my office.

I don't need her shit right now. I don't need it ever again. I was going to ask her to marry me until I learned that she was having extracurricular activities outside of our relationship. I never called her on it. Never made a big deal. I actually bought her a parting gift: a diamond bracelet, to soften the blow of our break up.

My shop is off limits right now, and so is my office. I step out onto the busy sidewalk and just start walking. I don't care about where I'm going. When I finally start paying attention, I realize I've walked the four blocks to my sister's apartment. I look up at the building and shrug my shoulders. I might as well go pay her a visit and spend some quality time with my niece.

"She smiled at me! I told you I'm her favorite uncle," I told my sister with a smile as I hold baby Jurnee in my arms.

"That's a gas smile. At best you're her second favorite uncle because she can't tell Draymond and Drummond apart. But they see her everyday, and you haven't seen her in how long?"

"Damn, you don't have to do me like that. I'm busy."I glare at her and fix my face back to a smile as I look down at the baby. She smiles again. "That's not gas. that's pure love and adoration," I tell my sister.

"Believe what you want, Dru. She's only six weeks old, and she hasn't started smiling socially just yet."

"I believe she just smiled socially three seconds ago,"I tell her pointing at the baby.

"I don't want to argue with you about this. You barely know where babies come from. Why are you here?"

"What do you think of Charisse?" I walk around the room holding the baby and avoiding eye contact with my sister.

"I think she's gorgeous. I think you light up when you're around her. And I think that you are good together." She has a warm smile on her face like the thought of me and Charisse together brings her joy.

I really want to tell her the truth, but I don't want to break my own NDA. She won't tell anybody though, and I really need her opinion on this.

"Can I tell you a secret?" I turn and look her straight in the eye.

"Please don't tell me your relationship with her is fake. Please.

Please." She's folding clothes and going about her regular life like she didn't just drop a bomb on me.

I can't speak. I open my mouth and nothing comes out, so I close it and look away.

"Oh my God! It is fake, you piece of shit. That's how you're trying to get around Mom's demands? I can't believe you. I really can't fucking believe you." She's dropped the onesie that she was folding and glares at me with her hands on her hips.

"I—" I have nothing to say. Nothing, so my sister keeps going.

"So why are you here?" she asks. Her scowl looks permanently tattooed on her face.

"Because I think I love her." I place the baby in her bassinet and sit down on the couch with my hands covering my face. "I think I have fallen in love with the woman that I'm paying to have a fake marriage with me, and I don't know how to get out of it or get in it or fix it or stop it." I take a shaky breath.

"If you love her, be with her. Break the contract that I know you had Hunter draw up. And just see where it goes. Maybe this can be an arranged marriage where people fall in love after they've been married." She laughs and sits down beside me, placing her hand on my knee. "You fucked this up. What were you thinking? And how on Earth did you think that you wouldn't fall in love with her? You pick a gorgeous, sweet, charismatic woman to be in a fake relationship with, and you're surprised when you actually fall in love with her? You're an even bigger fool than I thought you were. Does she feel the same way?"

"Yeah, she told me she was falling for me a few days ago, and I ran out of her apartment and sent her the first payment."

"Oh my God." She doesn't say anything else, just sits there

shaking her head at me, her eyes full of judgment and disappointment. "You need to do something nice for her. And you need to let her know how you feel. And you need to do it soon. She's going to internalize all of this, and you're going to miss your opportunity."

I take a deep breath and look at my sister. She's right. Every single thing that she said is right, and I'm the biggest fool on Earth if I screw this up any more than I already have. I stand up and place a kiss on her forehead. Then I walk over to the bassinet to place one on my niece's.

"I knew you were the one I needed to talk to. Thank you."

Chapter 19

Charisse

Dru hasn't texted me all day, and I feel bad about how we left things. This whole thing is more complicated than I thought it would be. There are too many complex feelings involved. I don't know what the solution is, but it's not us avoiding each other.

I drive to his office after school because I need to talk to him. I need to see him, actually. We were both so broken the last time we spoke, I need to know that he's okay.

I make my way to his office, and I'm greeted by a beautiful woman.

"Oh hi! You must be Dru's new assistant. I'm his fiancée Charisse. It's nice to meet you." I reach out my hand to shake hers, but she doesn't move. She just looks me up and down and scoffs.

"Um, okay," I say. I look around the office, but he's not here. "He's out," I say out loud because this lady is not listening to me.

"I'm supposed to marry him," she says to me with venom. "That heartfelt engagement was supposed to be mine. That rock on your finger was supposed to be mine. That man was supposed to be mine." She's trembling.

I don't know what to do about this. She's obviously not his

assistant. I wonder if she's an ex-girlfriend, or if she's a psychotic stalker that's here to murder me. When she crumbles into the chair and starts bawling, I lean more toward ex-girlfriend.

"So who are you?" I ask, trying to get a hold of this situation. I need a drop of context for this entire meltdown this lady's having right now.

"I'm Dru's ex-girlfriend, Khalia. He told me just a few minutes ago that he wanted to marry me. He's stuck with you now, and I don't know why he can't just break it with you and be with me where he belongs."

I didn't ask for all that. Did he tell her though? Does she know about our agreement? About our contract? I'm not going to bring it up, but I wonder how much truth there is in what she is saying.

"How long were you two together?" I ask, just being nosy at this point. She does seem like the type that he would go after. And I want to know more about this relationship they had.

"We were together for almost three years. He told me he loved me. I practically lived at his place. He wined and dined me, then he shattered my heart," she whines.

Maybe it's the whining that drove him away. I've only been talking to her for three minutes, and I want to burst my own eardrums.

"That's quite a long time."

"How long have you been together?" she asks me, accusation in her voice.

I cock my head to the side and try to figure it out. "A month? Maybe two?" The moment it leaves my mouth, I realize I should have not answered her question. And I was correct because she screams like she's being murdered. Now I feel really awkward. I'm not affected by her dramatics, but I don't want to be around this, so I do an about-face and walk right out of his office. I'll talk to Dru about this later or never.

"Are you pregnant?" Khalia yells as I step into the open elevator. The laughter that escapes me at her ridiculous question shakes my entire body. I'm laughing when I reach the ground floor, and I'm still laughing as I walk to my car and call Porsche.

"She asked you what?" Porsche squeals into the phone.

"You heard me," I tell her, laughing more.

"What an insult. What a bitchy thing to say. Where is she? Where does she work? I need to pay her a visit." Porsche has a bit of darkness in her voice.

"Leave her alone. That girl is just heartbroken about her lost bag. She's not in that office because she loves him and can't live without him. She's up there because someone else is stepping up into the money bags."

"You're right, but that doesn't mean I still don't want to beat her ass," Porsche tells me.

"I had no desire to beat her ass. I felt sorry for her. She was probably raised to marry a rich man and be his trophy wife, and whatever she did to fumble this bag is her own fault."

"Was she pretty at least?"

"Oh yeah. She was billboard pretty with a body to match. I felt a little inadequate when I looked at her, but I can tell her personality lacks substance. She couldn't even come up with a better reason why they should be together. I would have walked in there and had a whole closing argument about why we needed to still be together and why he needed to break his engagement. She had nothing but big boobs."

"You think they were fake?"

I laugh. Porsche is good for my soul. "Definitely fake."

"Everybody aint blessed with these natural, perky triple D's." I can see her bouncing her chest up and down as she says that, and I drop my phone laughing at her.

"Anyway girl, what else is going on with you and that man?"

"We haven't spoken since we got engaged." I try to keep my voice upbeat, but I know she can hear the wobble in it.

"That was yesterday. Do you usually talk in the morning or in the middle of the day, every single day? He's not your real man."

But I want him to be. I don't say that to her. I need to stop saying that to myself because it's not going to happen. He can have Khalia back when our time is up if he really wants to. It just wouldn't work out with us either way, not with us starting whatever we're calling this right now with a lie... a massive lie.

Back at my apartment, I sit down on my couch and stare at my bag full of essays. I need to hire an assistant to grade these for me. I have the money for it now. My motivation to do this is about $250,000 less than it was a week ago. I sigh and turn on a reality dating show and sit about my task.

Five essays into it, I give up. I graded five more than zero, but I can't take this right now. There's absolutely no punctuation in this sixth essay that I'm grading. What did this child learn his entire high school career? How is he a senior with no punctuation in a three-page essay? How is this a thing? Why am

I doing this?

I tossed the pile to the side and lean back on my couch, taking in the nonsense that is reality dating shows. The old me, the one from two months ago, would say that all these girls on the show are desperate. They go on this show on national television and compete for one man. But here I am, being paid to be in a fake relationship, so I'm not any better. I might be worse.

I pause the show when my phone rings. It's Dru.

"Hey," I say, trying to calm my enthusiasm. I'm happy he finally called me.

"How's your day been?" he asks.

"I went to your office after school today. You weren't there, but someone else was."

"Khalia?" He sounds stressed when he says her name.

"The one and only. She was having a bit of a fit. I don't think I helped when I answered her question about how long we've been together. You were going to marry her?"

"I was. Until I found her with her mouth gobbling down someone else's junk."

"Oh shit! That's not what I imagined broke you two up. I got to say that's a fairly valid reason to break it off with someone. What is she thinking trying to get you back right now?" I'm relieved. I didn't think her claim was legitimate, but knowing she was a cheater just makes me feel better. She deserves what she got.

"Yeah, I had the ring purchased and everything. I planned out an elaborate proposal, the whole nine. So as much as she wants to say I broke her heart, she really and truly broke mine."

"Damn, sorry. Cheating is the worst. I can't count how many times I've been cheated on. But I know I would never ever do that to someone. It makes you feel so unloved and so inadequate. Being cheated on really fucks with your head."

"It does. And it really did. If I'm being honest, that's part of why I asked you to do this with me. Putting my heart out there consciously was scary, and trusting someone again was something I didn't think I could do. It's so weird that all of that comes naturally between the two of us."

We're both silent for a while before he starts talking again. "What are you doing after school tomorrow?" he asked me.

"I'm not doing anything at all tomorrow, because there's no school." I definitely needed this break, and I'm so happy that it's finally here. I'm going to spend the next two days getting caught up, and then I'm going to spend the weekend resting.

"How long is your break?"

"Thursday and Friday, so I get a four-day weekend. I'm so excited to not have to do anything for the next four days if I don't want to."

"So you don't have plans for the next four days?" he asks. I can tell his wheels are turning.

"Not in the least," I tease, hoping he fills my days with something delightful.

"You do now. Be ready at 8:22 tomorrow morning."

"8:22?"

"8:00 a.m. was too early for you last time, so I'm giving you more time. Bring a little travel bag with your toiletries. That's the only hint you'll get."

"You're flying me out again?" I swoon. I can get used to this.

"I said that's the only hint you get. Don't be greedy. You'll see in the morning. Get some rest."

We end the call, and I can't take the smile off my face. It's not the money that has me feeling this way. It's not his ability to hop on a plane with no planning and no concerns. It's the fact that he wants to do this for me that makes my heart quicken.

I'm not going to get any sleep tonight. How can I when I'm going to be swept away in the morning to God knows where to do God knows what? He didn't even tell me what to pack. Well he said toiletries, so I'll listen. I'm so excited. I'm going to need melatonin to fall asleep.

Chapter 20

Charisse

At 8:20, I am sitting on my couch with my toiletry bag packed ready to be picked up. I can hear the car outside and his door shutting as he approaches. I wait for him to knock, but he doesn't. A full minute goes by, and he still doesn't knock. That tickles me so much that I run to the door laughing and pull it open.

"You were really hanging on to 8:22 a.m.," I tell him as I wrap my arms around him. He smells so good, and he looks delicious in his casual clothes. God bless the suit, but this man and some sweats makes me sweat.

"I wanted to make sure you had every minute of your time to get ready. I'm proud of you for being ready early." He kisses me on my cheek, takes my bag, and holds my hand as we walk to the car.

"I can't ask you any questions can I?" I tap my leg anxiously while we ride in the car.

He shakes his head, and a mischievous grin is on his face. I can accept a surprise, and I can wait until all is revealed to revel in whatever he has planned for us, for me. I can't shake this smile on my face, and I don't want to. I'm happy in this moment. I'm happy whenever I'm with him. And I don't want to think about anything else right now but that.

As expected, we arrive at the airport and pull all the way up to his family's jet. I still don't know where we're going, and my brain is creating narratives a mile a minute. Part of me thinks we're going somewhere tropical; another part thinks we're going somewhere cold and rustic. Could he take me out of the country? Do I need a passport for an international flight on a private jet? I shake my head. I'll never understand this life of the rich and famous. I'm going to have fun figuring it out.

"Did you eat?" Dru asks as we get settled into our seats.

"What do you think?" I look at him with a sly smile on my face.

"I know you didn't. You barely ever eat breakfast, so why would today be different?" He shakes his head at me, and I know he's about to give me the "breakfast is the most important meal of the day" speech— again, but he keeps his mouth shut and reaches behind him for a bag of fast food breakfast biscuits.

"Did you get me chicken biscuits?" I ask him, my excitement bubbling up to the surface.

"I believe we've discussed your favorite breakfast foods before, and you talked about how easy it is to travel with the chicken biscuit. How could I not get you chicken biscuits on the morning that you are traveling with me? Especially after you got ready on time. I'm really proud of you."

"Are you being sarcastic?" I ask, cutting my eyes at him.

He doesn't say anything, but he hands me a biscuit to make me happy and keep me quiet, and it works. I eat my biscuit quietly as the plane takes off, and I fall asleep the moment we hit 10,000 ft.

I don't know how long I've been asleep, but my body woke me

up as it felt us descending for landing. I like to fly, but the taking off and the landing make me feel a little anxious. Dru must have read that in my eyes because he reaches his hand out to mine across the aisle, and squeezes it the whole time until we land. I want to look over at him. I want to look into his eyes and see the feelings that I know he has for me growing, but I can't bring myself to do it. Any feelings that we have for each other are going to complicate and completely wreck what we're trying to do here. If we like each other now and try to actually build something, what happens if we have a horrible, ugly break up, but are still under contract for nine more months?I have to just stick it out. Maybe after this is all done, we can try something for real.

I finally look out the window and see the ocean. I don't know which ocean. I still have no idea where we are except that we are on the coast.

"Can you tell me where we are now?" I plead, batting my eyes at him.

"You haven't figured it out yet?" He's shaking his head in disappointment.

I look out the window again; it's the ocean. That's all I've got. Geography has never been on my radar. I can look up everything geographical that I need to know, so I tend to find which ocean I'm at has no purpose. Especially since I can't... couldn't afford to travel before.

"So you're still not going to tell me?" I ask. As we step out of the plane, I see sand and palm trees and the rest of the airport, and that gives me absolutely nothing.

"You are a smart lady, or so I thought. You should know right now where we are." He's just shaking his head at me, and there's a smile on his face that I kind of want to slap off.

I get smart instead, and pull out my phone. "Hey, where am I?" I ask my search app.

"Current location San Juan, Puerto Rico," my phone answers me.

I hold my phone up to Dru with a cocky look on my face. He crosses his arms and stares at me, waiting.

Once I'm done gloating, which is short-lived because he didn't even play along, I take in what my phone just said. We're in Puerto Rico. I can't remember if I mentioned it was on my bucket list during any of our conversations. I probably did because he is obviously the best listener I've ever met.

"I feel like I a-make-a-wish kid," I tell him. The air feels fresher here, and the breeze over the ocean tickles my skin. I don't want to ever go home, and we haven't even left the airport.

"That's incredibly insensitive," he scolds me.

"You're right. I'm sorry to everyone. Please don't make me leave." I need to stop talking before I say something else stupid. He may really put me back on the plane and send me back home.

"What made you do this for me?" I ask him. The airport traffic is light today, not that I have any idea how it usually is. The seas are parting for us as our driver maneuvers the roads.

"What makes you question that you deserve this?" he shoots back.

I stop gazing out the window and lean back in my seat, meeting his eyes. His intense eyes tear a hole in me.

"I'll talk to my therapist about that, thank you very much!" I huff.

He chuckles. "I did this for you because I want to see you smile. I haven't seen you truly relax since we met. It's been one worry after another. And I know this bit of pampering isn't erasing any worry you have for when you get back, but I'm hoping it'll push it down on your priority list. I'm hoping you'll let joy move in and stay for the next four days."

"My fiancé is the best guy in the whole world," I say to no one in particular.

Dru looks away from me, and I think it's a bit of sadness I see in his eyes. I don't push for more. I hit a nerve of some sort, and if he wants to talk to me about it, he will. I'm going to do what he asked of me and live in my joy for the next four days.

The resort is extraordinary. Not just run-of-the-mill fancy resort. It drips in luxury and screams filthy rich. Exotic and fragrant flowers bloom on every inch of land. There's a mix of fancy but also a love of nature that's obvious. Everywhere I look, there is something new and beautiful to behold. The sun feels different here; it's gently caressing my skin instead of burning me to a crisp as it should be at this time of day.

So many thoughts flood my mind when we enter the lobby to check in. I first wonder if we are sharing a room or sharing a bed.

"Mr. Martin. Welcome to Flor Del Playa. We are so happy to have you here. Thank you for choosing to stay here. Our presidential suite is prepared with the specifications your assistant gave us. I hope you and your fiancée have a beautiful stay." The young woman at the front desk tells him. She smiles warmly at me.

"Assistant?" I ask him as we make our way to the room empty-handed. The bellhop has the bags Dru packed. I'm carrying only my purse that I was smart enough to load up with my daily meds, my toothbrush, and a change of underwear.

"After both of our run-ins with Khalia, I figured I need a friendly guard to at least warn me of incoming danger." Having your cheating ex-girlfriend run up on you should make you pause and reconsider your choices.

"Smart thinking," I tell him. His five o'clock shadow is coming in, and it's really sexy on him. "Have you ever thought of growing a beard?" I ask him, unable to take my eyes off his face.

He rubs his hand on his chin and scratches at the stubble. "No, I'm a clean-shaven kind of guy. Did you really have to ask me that?"

"You can't get it to connect, can you?" I tease.

He bursts into laughter and rubs his chin again. "Woman, I damn sure can get it to connect. I want to be smooth, that's all." He turns away from me and opens the door to the presidential suite. My jaw hits the ground when I step inside. The whole wall has floor-to-ceiling windows, and a view of the entire coastline on this side of the island.

"I'm in a coma," I say. "This isn't my real life. I'm on life support in a coma, and the sun is going to hit just right in a minute, and I'll step into the light." Tears well up in my eyes. I don't get to live like this. I don't get to do these kinds of things. I eat noodles for dinner more times in a week than I care to admit. I can't manage money to save my fucking life, and here I am in the presidential suite after stepping off a private jet in Puerto Rico. I was teaching seniors to capitalize the word "I" yesterday.

Dru rushes toward me and supports my weight because my knees are weak.

"You're about to have a panic attack. Take a deep breath, and tell me what color the couch is," he whispers to me.

Air fills my lungs, and I look at the couch. It's seven different colors. "It's a kaleidoscope of colors. I can't just tell you one. It's the most complicated upholstery pattern I've ever seen."

Dru loosens his hold on me and laughs. "Ok, she's back." He walks me to said couch, and we sit down together.

"Why are you being weird?" Dru asks me, and he's dead serious. He's known that I'm weird for the past couple of months. I agreed to marry him for money, didn't I?

"You're just now realizing that about me?" Something's wrong with him. I've been who I am from the moment I met him, I don't know who he thought I was going to turn into, but I'm consistently myself. "Anyway, what are the plans for the next four days? I know you have an agenda, so go ahead and send it to my phone. I'll try to be on time to every activity and be appropriately dressed. Did you bring me clothes? Did you buy me clothes? All I have packed is a pair of panties."

His eyebrows shoot up, and he smiles at me seductively.

"That's not a part of our agreement kind sir. I'm down if you are, but it'll cost you double. I'm going to be a high dollar hoe. You can't get this for free." I stand up and run my hand down my body.

He shakes his head at me. It's like his favorite thing to do, and it's super judgmental. but we all have our flaws, so I let it go.

"We don't have any plans." He pauses and looks at me thoughtfully. "This isn't our vacation. It's your vacation, so we do whatever you want when you want."

I cross my arms and rub my chin with my hand. "Whatever I want?"

"If you want some of this, it goes both ways so something's coming out of your check." His face is serious. It doesn't falter at all, meanwhile I am squealing with laughter.

This is going to be a fun trip. I want to jam pack this trip with every activity I've ever wanted to do, but never thought that I could. I want to zipline. I want to jump off a waterfall. I want to scuba dive. I brainstorm, trying to think up the most extreme vacation excursions that I can, because Dru is paying for every last one of them, and I'm going to milk him.

Chapter 21

Dru

I excuse myself to the bathroom while Charisse tours the suite. She's as happy as a kid on Christmas. Her reaction is new for me because the women I'm used to dating expect all of this. Nothing surprises them, and sometimes what I do isn't enough. Charisse takes it all in, and that's fun to see. It makes me want to do more for her. She may be marrying me for money, but that's not all she sees in me. That's not why she likes me.

This whole time, Charisse has been getting to know me, the man, and not me, the multi-millionaire. This whole time I've been trying to lead with money and keep feelings out of it, but I have these feelings, and I think she deserves to know.

I have an idea when I come out of the bathroom, but I need some time to execute it.

"Charisse," I call out as I step into the sitting area.

"There's only one bed," she tells me from the bedroom.

"I know."

"Oh." She pauses, then bounces back. "What's up?"

"I'm sending you shopping. The lobby has a list of stores, and the driver will take you to any of them or all of them. Charge whatever you want to my name."

Her mouth falls open, but she recovers quickly.

"I like your surprise reactions. You don't have to suppress them."

"Oh, you like being Daddy Money Bags?" she asks.

"Call me Daddy again," I dare her, meaning it. I will take her right here if she says it again. She just laughs instead and winks at me.

"Dru," she says, pointedly. "I'm heading down to the lobby now to go on a magnificent shopping spree. Just for grins and giggles, what's my spending limit? I doubt I'll go anywhere near it, but just tell me for fun."

I step close to her, so close I can smell the coconut and almond oil in her hair. "There is no limit. Buy as much as you like. If you buy so much that it won't fit on the plane, we will ship it. Don't forget to get some jewelry. Find some unique pieces that no one back home will have ever seen."

She sucks in a breath.

"I mean it. Buy a $10,000 ring for yourself. Buy whatever you want." I hold on to her elbow and press a kiss on her cheek.

"Thank you," she whispers and leaves the suite.

I know she's not going to do any of that. At best, she'll spend $3,000. I send a text to Roxanne, the woman manning the front desk and have her send a personal shopper to trail Charisse to buy the things she looks at and reconsiders because they're too expensive.

Then I sit at the desk and work on part two of my plan.

Hours later, Charisse strolls into the suite with the biggest sun hat ever made on her head. The bellhop pushes a luggage cart full of shopping bags, and his arms are full too. The look on Charisse's face tells me she's shopped her heart out.

I quickly check the balance on the card I sent the personal shopper with, and as I thought, she spent less than $3,000.

"How'd it go?" I ask, taking some of the bags from the bellhop and slipping him a generous tip.

"That was so much fun!" she squeals, spinning around in a circle wearing a new sundress. It shows just enough skin with a peek-a-boo cutout in the back and the front with a twirly skirt and spaghetti straps.

"Should we put on a fashion show after dinner?" I ask her. It takes all of my self-control to not touch her. I want to touch the smooth skin on her back. It would be nothing to slip my hand in that cutout. It's inviting me too. That's not what this weekend is about. It's about her and making her happy, not fulfilling my base needs.

"We can do whatever after dinner. I am starving. A full day of shopping will do that to a girl." She plops down on the couch dramatically, and I just smile at her. She's so adorable right now. I can't take it. I just want to sit here with her all day and get to know her more. I want to spend the next four days making her smile and making her happy and bringing her joy. I need to figure out how to do that without money. All I've been doing is throwing money at her, and I need to start trying to figure out how to spend time with her.

"What are you thinking about for dinner?" I ask her, hoping she says something that I like.

"I honestly don't know anything about the cuisine here. I trust your judgment. So take me to your very favorite place ever."

She must have just read my mind. I smile at her and kiss her on the cheek. That was probably cheek kiss number twenty. But I can't play games with her. I can't tempt myself further. We have to keep our boundaries well defined, even if I have a hard time keeping my hands off her.

"What was that for?" she asks me as she brings her hand to her cheek. A smile spreads across her face, and she looks at me with an expression I've never seen before.

"I was just hoping you'd say that because I have the best place to go to. It's my favorite restaurant ever." I'm practically bouncing on my toes.

"Ever? Don't tell me anything then, and let's play a game. I'll read the menu and guess what your favorite dish is. And you guess what I plan to order." Her smile brightens up the whole space we're in.

"Deal!" I shake her hand. "Go change into the most expensive dress you bought. This place is fancy."

She rummages through the bags. "There's more here than I bought," she says.

"I didn't buy this. I tried it on, but it—"

"Was it expensive?" I finish her sentence.

"Yeah, how'd you know?" She holds the dress up and admires it. It looks expensive. I know it'll look exquisite on her.

"I sent an extra helper to follow you around and buy the things you put back because you thought they were too expensive."

"You knew I'd be frugal?" She puts her hands on her hips and purses her lips. I make fists with my hands and slip them in my pockets. Those lips. I take a quiet, deep breath.

"Weren't you?" I ask, knowingly.

"Well, yes. I don't know what it means to buy whatever I want."

"It's pretty self-explanatory."

"You know what I mean."

I nod. "You don't want to take advantage, and I love that about you. Most women I've spent time around would ball the hell out and not think twice about it. You're a rare gem, and you deserve to be spoiled and pampered."

"Dru, I'm just poor. That's really all this is." Her shoulders sag a little.

"No, you have integrity. That counts for a lot. But I snuck behind your back and got you everything you really wanted." I cross my arms over my chest and lean against the wall.

Her eyes get big. "Oh shit."

"You just remembered something you tried on?" I ask, my smile so big it hurts. I don't know what she's thinking of, but I know when she sees it in these bags, she's going to freak out. My heart races in anticipation.

She drops to her knees and digs through the bags until she pulls up the smallest dark blue bag from the premier jeweler in San Juan. She's wiggling with excitement while she takes the small ring box out. She drops the bag on the floor and just marvels at the velvet square case.

"Open it woman! I want to know what it is!"

"No, you don't. This was so expensive. I don't even know why I tried it on. I guess I was just dreaming." She sighs and opens the box. Inside there is a ring with a solitary yellow diamond. It's probably four or five carats. I'd have to get a closer look. I'm sure it was an easy $20,000.

"Good choice! My sister loves colorful diamonds. She has a whole collection." I walk over to her and take the ring out. It's definitely five carats.

"I can't accept this." She closes the lid , stands, and hands it to me. "We need to take this back."

I chuckle. "They don't refund $20,000 rings."

"It was $30,000," she whispers.

"It must be damn near perfect. This is a collector's piece. You have a good eye!" I take her right hand and slide the ring on her ring finger. It fits perfectly. "See that. It's meant to be." I bring her hand to my mouth and place a kiss on it.

Dammit, another kiss. I really can't help it though. She's so... Charisse.

"I can't accept a $30,000 ring." She takes it off and shakes her head.

"You do realize the one on your left hand was $70,000, right? I thought I was being cheap with it too. As my wife-to-be and when you're my wife, you'll be expected to know and love the luxurious life. Lean into it, Charisse. Even if this is all fabricated, you do deserve nice things. I'm going to shower you with them now until you get used to it."

"I'll never get used to owning a piece of jewelry that costs more than I make in a year. I just don't think I can."

"If you make less than $70,000 for what you do, then you definitely deserve to wear that much on your hand. Charisse, you work hard. And you're the best woman I've ever met. Let me spoil you. Let me buy you ridiculously expensive things."

She looks at me and doesn't say a thing.

"So, put on that sexy, expensive dress along with that 30K ring that matches the dress so well, that it's meant to be. And let's go enjoy my favorite restaurant."

Chapter 22

Charisse

The ring on my finger feels heavier now that I know it's a $70,000 ring. I cannot believe I've been wearing it over these past few days without thinking about how much it costs. I can't understand why Dru is doing all of this. He told me it's expected of me to live in luxury. I just don't know how to. I don't know how I'll convince everyone that I'm meant to be with him over the next year and a half. I can't get used to having so much money spent on me. It hurt me today to spend the $2,500 I did on the things I purchased.

It's really sweet that he knew I'd cheat, so he sent a spy. It's much more sweet than creepy. I was so wrapped up in shopping that I didn't notice I was being trailed. Today was fun. I still bought with little caution. If it had been my money, I would have bought a single dress and nothing more. This insane sun hat would have stayed in the store. I wouldn't have tried it on. I didn't know I had a hat head until today.

My travel coconut oil comes through in the clutch because my skin is dry, and I can't mess up this look. I smooth it all over my exposed skin, and it makes me shine. I shimmy into the new dress the spy bought for me. It's so revealing and silky. Dru's going to lose his mind when he sees me in it. He's been very touchy-feely with me today. I'm curious what this dress will do to his resolve. I'm not trying to go past our lines, but I do love teasing a man and watching him squirm.

My one splurge when I was shopping were the shoes I'm about to put on. I knew they cost more than I'd ever spend on shoes, but I had to have them. They complement this dress just as well as this yellow diamond ring does. When I look in the mirror, I barely recognize myself. I look the part I'm playing.

As usual, they know exactly who Dru is when we enter, so we are escorted to the premier table in the restaurant. It's not in a secluded area. Instead, it's where everyone can see us. I don't know how I feel about this, but I'll go with the flow.

"I already know you're going to get the shrimp," I tell him after I've read the whole menu. He has some kind of seafood fetish, and shrimp is his very favorite.

He doesn't say anything. He just laughs and laughs, and it's a beautiful sound. All eyes are on us too, because he's loud.

"Do you know what you want?" he asked me. I grin and nod. He's going to get this right because I eat the same thing all the time.

"So, I can guess now?"

"Yeah go ahead, you already know what it is. Go ahead and say it and be right," I tease him.

"I'll wait till the waiter gets here, so it's a high-pressure situation. You won't be allowed to order anything else. You have to eat what I order." He looks at me with mischief in his eyes.

"You better get it right," I scold him. "I will make a scene up here in front of all these people who know who you are and have no idea who I am."

He fakes a wince and laughs.

The waiter comes right on time and Dru orders himself the shrimp. He motions for the waiter to lean down closer, and he whispers my order in the waiters here.

"Oh my God! You're doing it like that?"

"Is there any other way?" He eyes me and a wicked grin is on his face.

I take a deep breath, and tell myself to let this man take the lead. He's not going to do anything to jeopardize this good time we're having. He's going to order me some delicious food, and I'm going to love it, and I cannot get upset about this.

"You look ravishing tonight," he tells me, obviously trying to change the subject.

"Indeed, Charisse Turner sponsored by Dru Martin." I wave my hand in the air so that this gorgeous yellow diamond catches the light.

"You don't have to bring that up," he tells me, turning serious.

I can't tell if he's angry or not, so I sit in silence.

"I know you feel weird about having money spent on you, and I know you don't think you fit into the life that I live, but you do. You fit into my life in a way that no one has ever fit in before, and nothing brings me more joy than to spend money on someone I truly appreciate."

I don't know what to say, so I just nod and take a sip of my water. The waiter appears with a pina colada. I sigh in relief because I need a drink.

"If this is any indication of how you ordered for me, you're right on track.," I tell him before I take a long sip of the drink.

"I'm not going to do you wrong. Why would I mess up a perfectly great day? And I know how you are about your food. I ordered the perfect meal for you. Just wait and see."

Stuffed from what will now be known as the greatest meal I have ever eaten in my life: shrimp mofongo with spicy tomato sauce, I walk beside Dru to our suite. I only had one drink, so I'm not too gone. I am buzzed; there's no denying that.

"You can barely walk," Dru teases me, his hand braced on my back.

"I ate like an animal," I confess, almost out of breath from this movement and my full stomach.

"Let's get you to bed then,"he tells me while he opens the door to our suite.

"Bitch!"

My heart skips a beat at the familiar voice and the familiar moniker I hear. It takes a minute for me to focus and really see that Porsche and Lily are standing in the entryway to our presidential suite.

"What?" That's all I have. I can't say anything else. I can't move. I turn to Dru. "Did you orchestrate this?"

"You think we did?" Porsche asks, shaking her head at me.

"Leave me alone," I tell her, still frozen.

"Imagine my shock when I got a phone call four hours ago telling me to pack a bag and be ready for three days on an island,"

Porsche tells me. Lily stands beside her, nodding in agreement. "Now, you know I wasn't going to say no. And since it was your boo, I wasn't even going to ask any questions. I just did what I was told and sat out on my stoop like a child who forgot her key, waiting for Chance to come and pick me up." Porsche smiles, radiating joy, and I love seeing this.

Lily is a little more reserved, just as I would expect her to be. "I had to cancel a paint and sip, but Dru promised to make it up to me. And if you can't trust your best friend's fake fiancé, who can you trust?"

"Wow!" Dru responds.

Lily shrugs, and we all burst into laughter. I turn to Dru "What made you do this?"

"We don't look a gift horse in the mouth," Porsche tells me, wagging her finger.

"Hush," I tell her and turn back to Dru. "Really, what made you do this?"

"You deserve it. And anyone who loves you deserves it too."

"That's a good man, Savannah," Porsche says, dabbing away a fake tear.

"You are so ridiculous," I tell her through my laughter.

"So what are the arrangements?" Lily asks, getting down to business.

"I know y'all are in a fake relationship and all, but I don't want to share a suite with you two. Who knows if something might pop off, if the mood is right? I'm not one to be a blocker, so don't have me up here with you."

My face heats up, and I look away from everyone. My shoes are suddenly the most interesting thing in the room, then the wall and the painting that adorns it piques my interest.

"That was a mouthful," Dru tells her, a deep chuckle coming out of him. "You two are actually a floor above us in the penthouse. There's a balcony, hot tub,and even an infinity pool that overlooks the ocean." He steps forward to hand them both their keys. "We have plans for the evening. There are gifts on your bed for you, use them and meet us back down here in an hour."

He handles Porsche well and doesn't even blink at her nonsense. I think he's shocked Lily mute. She said very few words, and she's having a hard time processing this. That's where she and I are similar. Porsche takes as much as she can, and I love that about her. She knows how to relax, how to be pampered and how to be adored. It all just makes me uncomfortable.

"You didn't have to do this." I tell Dru when we're alone.

"I know," he tells me. "But I wanted to. And I can. So I did."

I can't take this smile off my face. He did all of this for me. It's one thing to sweep me off my feet, but to fly my friends out and get them their own hotel room? That's a different ballpark. That's a different galaxy. I take a deep breath and let it out slowly. He takes my hand and squeezes it.

"There's a gift for you too on the bed. How about you freshen up and use the gift, and meet me out here when you're done?"

Thirty minutes later, I step out of the bathroom in the most luxurious silk pajamas that I've ever felt in my life. I sit beside him on the couch.

"Do you like them?" He asks, running his hand along my thigh.

I'm sure he's feeling the material up and not me, but either way, I let him.

"I love these. They're so comfortable and soft, and this orange is so vibrant." I place my hand on my thigh and feel the material myself, and his hand rests on mine. I look up at him, and he's staring right in my face. Something comes over me, and I lean toward him. He leans in, and we both hear the key card being inserted into the door and jump back from each other.

"Damn, I probably should have knocked first, huh?" Porsche says, cackling at our wide-eyed expressions.

"You're sure she's your best friend?" Dru asks me, shooting a playful glare at Porsche. She and Lily don the same pajamas as me but in black.

"These are so comfortable, Dru. Thank you." Lily says when she walks in. "And the room is on another level. I've never been in a hotel room with an infinity pool. They're so relaxing."

"It's truly my pleasure. I want to show all of you ladies a good time," he says, staring right at me.

"I'm not really into sharing men, but I'll make an exception just this once," Porsche says as she plops down on the couch next to Dru.

I stare at her with my mouth wide open. I know this is who she is, but this is way too much.

"As beautiful as you both are, when I'm in a relationship, fake or real, I stick with just one woman. It's just too bad you didn't want me to sit next to you at the paint and sip that day." Dru stands up, and stretches. " I'm going to go shower and put my pajamas on, and we'll get to know each other a little better." He slips into the bedroom and closes the door.

It's not completely latched closed before Porsche goes in. "You have to marry him for real, girl. I need to live this life on the regular. You are in the presidential suite. Yesterday, you were in your one-bedroom apartment that is smaller than this hotel room. Marry that man."

I gape at her, understanding what she's saying, but also lost. It doesn't work like that.

Lily finally comes to life and sits down beside me. "This is unbelievable. I really can't believe this is happening to me because of you. I can't believe that you are in such a wonderful relationship with a wonderful man, and it's all fake. I think that's why I'm so quiet. You do deserve all of this. He's right. But it's all farce, and just when you start getting used to it, it's going to be over. He's perfect for you. Absolutely perfect for you, and this business deal you have going is ruining everything."

"Way to lay that shit on heavy," Porsche says, shaking her head at Lily. "We all know what the facts are about this whole thing. But we can put the facts in the back of our minds and focus on this free ass vacation that none of us will ever be able to afford. We got flewed out on a PJ. On a motherfucking PJ. We left the country without going through security. I don't even know if I have my ID on me right now. For however long this lasts is how long you need to enjoy every damn moment of it. You do deserve this shit. We all do. But you got it first."

"All right ladies," Dru says as he comes out of the bathroom. He's wearing basketball shorts and a tank top, and it's more skin than I've ever seen on him. His chest is bigger than I thought, and the tattoos gracing it beg to be explored.

"I did NOT think you'd be tatted up, Mr. Executive," Porsche exclaims, speaking my mind for me.

"That goes to show you don't know me at all. I'm Mr. Executive when I need to be, and I'm just Dru any other time." He sits down beside me and lifts my legs into his lap.

"Ok, Just Dru. What's on the agenda for tonight," Porsche asks.

"Board games. He pulls the surface of the coffee table forward and reveals a compartment full of games. He rummages for a bit then takes out the box of tower blocks.

"This one is my favorite," Lily says, speaking for the first time since Dru reentered.

"It's because you have those steady painting hands, isn't it?" I ask, already knowing my clumsy self is going to knock the whole thing down on my first move.

"This version has a twist. We all answer the questions on the blocks as we restack them." He holds up a block to show us the question on it.

"Ooh, this is going to be fun!" Lily claps.

Dru sets the game up with Lily while Porsche and I head to the bar to get wine for all of us. When we return, Porsche pours everyone a glass of wine, and we settle into playing.

Lily easily removes and replaces the first block. "What's the biggest wild animal you think you could beat in a fight?" she reads, then giggles into her wine. We all turn to Dru because he's the man of the group, and we know he's going to be overly confident.

"The biggest?" He pauses, taking a slow sip from his glass. "A goat," he says, matter-of-fact.

"A goat?" all three of us say in unison. I was expecting him to say a bear or a mountain lion. This man said a goat.

"Let me explain. They aren't super aggressive. I mean, they can headbutt and all that, but they don't get so big that I can't pick it up and body slam it." He motions what he'd do to it, and I squeal with laughter.

He looks to Porsche, who he seems to enjoy antagonizing, and raises his eyebrows.

"Me? Oh, a deer, for sure." She crosses her arms over her chest definitively.

"Explain," he says.

"Have you seen their little peg legs? One good kick or even punch, and that thing is splitting in two. Then it's on and popping. I'm kicking that deer's ass." She karate chops the air with both hands. Dru loses it and erupts into laughter.

"What's so funny? Jealous that my animal is bigger than yours?" she challenges.

He holds up his hands and shakes his head, still laughing. "No! I just envisioned you beating a deer's ass. It makes perfect sense. I saw the whole thing: the broken leg and all of your moves. It's wild!"

"Yeah, yeah. Wifey, whose ass would you kick?" she asks me.

I spent too much time listening and laughing. I haven't thought of anything. "A koala," I say, confidently.

Dru and Porsche howl with laughter, tears streaming down their faces.

"Why would you be in a fight with a koala?" Lily asks, horror painted across her face.

"I don't know. Why would they fight a deer or a goat? This question is meant to be ridiculous," I argue.

"No, your answer is out there," Dru says. He rubs my leg affectionately, but I see the judgment in his eyes.

"Lily, it's your turn," I announce, pouting.

"I think I could wrangle an alligator," she says, looking thoughtful like she's planning the attack out.

"Bitch, what?" Porsche yells. "An alligator? That's that white blood in you seeping out. I knew it was in there somewhere with your lite brite ass."

We burst out laughing.

Through her own laughter, Lily tries to explain. "Look, I saw a girl do it in a video."

"Was she white?" Porsche asks.

"Do you really need to ask?" I add.

"Shut up, both of you. I saw her just jump on its back and hang on while planting her feet on the ground. She got its mouth tied all the way up without being eaten." She finishes.

"And you think because you saw it in a video, that you'd be able to do it too?" Dru asks, amused.

"In this fantasy world where we're all beating up wild animals? Yeah."

We have this much fun whenever we're together, and it's so nice that adding Dru to the mix changes nothing. I watch him interact with my friends, and pure happiness is all I feel.

He walks them up to their hotel room at the end of the night. I stay behind and get ready for bed. Today's been the best day of my whole year. The only anxiety I felt was at the idea of spending too much of Dru's money. In the end, I spent too little. What a life!

I don't know if I could get used to this, but I sure do enjoy it.

Chapter 23

Dru

When the ladies finally leave around 1 a.m., I'm ready to go to sleep. Orchestrating all of this has been exhausting, and I'm ready to lay down. Charisse and I head to the bedroom, wordlessly. Neither of us sure about these sleeping arrangements at this point. I'm of the thought that we'll both be too tired to consider the implications of our sleeping in the same bed together, even though that's what I'm doing now. I'd pay a fortune to know what she's thinking at the moment.

"What's on your mind?" I ask her anyway, hoping to get an honest, unfiltered answer.

"I'm thinking about how awkward it is to be sleeping in the bed with you," she says bluntly.

I wanted honesty, and I got it. I laugh and agree with her, although awkward isn't quite what I was thinking. There's an angel and a devil on my shoulders right now. One's telling me to take my ass to sleep because I have three women to entertain tomorrow. The other is telling me that Charisse and I have more energy in us to spend a few more hours awake.

I'm listening to the angel and facing the wall on my side of the bed. I crawl into the bed with good intentions. I refuse to complicate things with physicality that neither of us can handle right now. I think we've got something brewing between us that we're both actively trying to ignore. Pushing that boundary tonight will send us over the edge.

"Dru, today was such a perfect day. Never in my wildest dreams would I have imagined everything that happened. Thank you," she tells me. She's laying on the left side of the bed, on her side—facing me.

I turn to face her, resting one of my arms under my head. "I enjoyed it too. Your friends are hilarious, and it was nice to see you smile so much," I tell her.

"My face hurts from smiling so hard all day long." She rubs on her jaw, smiling more.

"Really?" I reach across the bed and touch her face. She sighs and closes her eyes at my touch. I don't know what makes me do it, but that one touch was too much for me. I move closer to her until our faces are just inches apart.

"It's nothing I can't handle. Smile pain is a good pain to have." She gazes into my eyes, and my resolve disappears. I close in the distance between us and kiss her. It's just a small peck, but her body shudders when our lips touch, letting me know she wants to do this as much as I do.

"Are you sure?" I ask. I don't want to assume she consents to this based on a sigh and shudder.

"Yes. I want you, Dru," she whispers. She reaches up around the back of my neck, pulling me closer and kissing me deeper, opening her mouth and inviting my tongue in. I'm seized by an urge to feel her skin against mine. As I run my hand along her neck, she takes a deep breath, and a tingle of anticipation rolls through me. She moves her hand around my waist, sliding it under my shirt. I help her get my shirt off, then I set to the take of slowly unbuttoning her silky pajama shirt.

My fingers brush against her smooth skin as I carefully open each button, peeling open the fabric with a gentle tug to reveal her shoulder blades. She moves closer into my chest as I kiss the exposed parts of her neck, softly, tenderly releasing another shudder from her.

My breath is ragged with desire. We have nothing but time, so I keep my slow pace, savoring every moment. She slides off one side of her shirt, exposing more of her beautiful curves. She takes one of my hands, guiding it across the valley between her breasts. Her heart races.

I take in a slow, deep breath, and lower my mouth to her breast, pushing the rest of the fabric away with my nose. Her nipple peaks, waiting for me. When my tongue touches it, she melts. A moan with the power to bring me to my knees sounds throughout the room, making me happy I put her friends on a different floor of the hotel. The sounds I want to hear from her aren't for anyone else's ears.

"I didn't know you made those sounds," I whisper with my mouth hovering over her nipple, my breath brushing against it. She moans again.

"Keep doing that, and I'll sing for you." She breathes, her hands clawing at me.

I lap at her nipple again and again, making her writhe underneath me.

"Are you wet for me?" I ask her, sliding my hand down her body and slipping my hand into her pants. I inhale deeply. "You're not wearing anything under this?" My dick just got rock hard.

She moans and shakes her head.

I slide my hand down more, avoiding her clit—saving it for last. I trail my fingers along her folds until I reach my destination and almost lose my shit. She's dripping wet. I want to rip these pants off and take her now.

Control. I have to maintain my control and do this right.

"Shit, girl." I clamp down on her nipple and slip my fingers inside of her. "You feel so good." I tell her with a mouthful of her.

"I taste even better," she breathes, bucking her hips at my touch.

"Oh really?" I ask, pulling away from her.

She sits up, panting, and looks at me with wild eyes. "What are you doing?"

I tug at her bottoms, pulling them all the way off, then I gaze at her in all her glory. "I'm preparing to ravish you. I want to see how you taste, then I want to fuck you until you're hoarse."

She lays back down, her eyes hooded, and spreads her legs apart which makes my dick just about burst out of my bottoms. I lean forward and drag my tongue along her stomach, eliciting another moan from her. I run my hands up and down her sides as I work my way lower. When I reach her inner thigh, I lick from one side to the other in slow circles until she's trembling with anticipation, coming so close to her clit but still avoiding it. She shifts around impatiently, begging for more. Heedless of her pleas, I continue down and then back up until finally teasing my way to her pussy.

Words fail me as I take in the sight of her glistening core and her legs trembling with the force of her desire. I continue running my tongue along the inside of her thigh slowly, teasing her. She whimpers, begging. I do a few more runs, coming dangerously close to her clit before burying my face between her legs. My mouth plays over every inch of flesh that it touches, focusing on her entrance, thrusting my tongue inside of her and holding her hips tightly as she shudders.

"Dru." She moans my name and arches her back, her head coming completely off the bed. Now. I have to dive all the way in right now, so I zero in on my target—her pulsing clit—making sure to make true on my promise to leave her hoarse.

I lap my tongue at her with agonizing slowness, starting from the bottom and dragging it up to the top where I flick at her clit softly. She sucks in a breath and holds it. I do it again, bottom to top, but this time I gently suck on her clit, and she groans, coming up off the bed again.

"Goddamn, Dru," she moans before falling back against the pillows. Again, I drag my tongue up, but this time I slide my fingers inside of her. She clamps on them immediately, and I curl them, searching for that spot.
"Oh," she cries out, and I know I've found it, so I stay on it: moving my fingers and tongue in synchrony. She's so far gone that no sounds come out of her. She's panting and writhing at my touch, and I'm about to bust in my pants.

"Give it to me," she says in between her ragged breaths. "I want it now!"

I look up at her, my mouth still on her clit, sucking it. I briefly let up to answer her. "Not yet. You haven't come for me yet." I wrap my whole mouth around her clit and slide my tongue up one side and down the other, over and over again until her body tightens. "That's right," I say with my mouth full of her. I keep on her until a scream explodes. Her body trembles as she comes in my mouth.

"Yes, let it out. Now you're ready for me," I tell her as I grab a condom from the drawer beside the bed and put it on. Her eyes double in size when she sees my dick. If she thinks it looks good, she's in for it when she realizes how good I'm about to make her feel.

"Are you ready?" I ask before I enter her.

"Yes, please. Yes," she pleads as she shimmies down the bed.

"Don't move. I'll come to you," I tell her, crawling closer to her while I stroke my dick. I could come right now just at this sight, with the taste of her still on my tongue. I hover over her, and her hands are all over me, trying to guide me in. I don't move at her urging. Instead, I reach for her breast and cup it in my hand, then I bring my mouth down and place it over her nipple.

Her head rolls back, and her mouth falls open. Another silent sigh escapes her. While her eyes are closed, and she's wrapped up in the ecstasy of what my tongue is doing to her nipple, I slowly slide into her. She stiffens and looks at me with wide eyes.

"I'm going to take it slow and make sure you coat me first before I go all the way in. I got you," I whisper in her ear.

She relaxes, and I slide in a little more. Her breathing becomes rapid, and I can feel what I'm doing to her walls. I slide out a little, and she exhales, then I slip back in, further this time. She groans. I do it again, coating my dick in her juices, so I can slide all the way in.

I keep my thrusts shallow so she can get used to my size. She's not hoarse yet, but she's speechless. I don't want a quiet fuck, so I have some work to do. When I can feel that she's ready, I go in deep, almost losing myself in how good she feels.

Her nails dig into my back. I thrust faster, holding myself up with one arm while my other hand palms her breast and rubs her nipple with my thumb. Her eyes are closed, and she moans my name in a way I've never heard before.

"You can't be making sounds like that," I whisper in her ear as I nip her earlobe, still thrusting into her.

"I can't help it," she cries out, arching her back and thrusting her hips to meet my stroke.

"Damn!" I hiss, trying to maintain my composure and hold in the moan trying to make its way out of me. "You got me wanting to yell, Charisse."

"Say my name again," she pants.

"Charisse," I say through gritted teeth.

"Mmmm, I like that." She bucks her hips at me hard, and my arm slips. I almost collapse on top of her, but I catch myself and grab her arms, pinning them above her head and staring into her eyes while I stroke her hard and slow.

"You're not in charge here." I kiss her mouth, thrusting my tongue into her mouth, then biting her bottom lip gently. She tries to move her arms, but I hold them down, so she bucks her hips more, riding me from the bottom.

"What are you trying to do?" I groan, struggling to keep my eyes open, pleasure rippling through me.

"Fucking you until you're hoarse," she says, smiling.

I bend down again and take her nipple into my mouth, nibbling on it this time. She moans my names and goes rigid, her walls clamping around me.

"Yes, Charisse. Come for me."

She's holding her breath, trying to hold it in. I nibble on her nipple more and slide almost all the way out before slamming into her. "You can do it. Come for me baby."

"Let yourself go," I coax as my hips meet hers with each insistent thrust. Her muscles quiver beneath my touch, and her eyes flutter open to reveal a sight of raw ecstasy.

"Can't...hold..." she stuttered, her voice barely audible over the thunderous heartbeat pounding in my ears.

"That's right, Charisse," I breathe. With one final, powerful push, her body convulses under me in answer to my command.

Her grip tightens around me as she cries out in pleasure, the sweet release exploding from within her.

I feel my own climax building, the pressure mounting inside me. I grit my teeth against the overwhelming sensation that threatens to consume me. My strokes become erratic, driven by a primal need for release. I can feel the tension coiling tighter inside me: a spring wound too hard and desperate to snap.

"Charisse," I groan, my hands gripping her hips with such force that it'll surely leave a mark. The sound of skin against skin fills the room, mixing with our ragged breaths.

"I know," she gasps back, reading my need in my eyes. Her nails dig deeper into my back as she arches against me even harder. "Please."

My control shatters completely at her pleading tone. "Charisse," I moan again as an intense wave of pleasure crashes over me. My body stiffens as I drive into her one final time, surrendering to the overwhelming sensation that rips through me.

Chapter 24

Charisse

When Porsche and Lily lay eyes on me the next morning over breakfast, they giggle and exchange a look. Do I look sexed up?

Dru sent us down to the hotel restaurant to eat everything we wanted while he readied plans for today's excursions. Or so he could sleep off the sex stupor he was in. He exhausted us both last night. We went for several rounds before we collapsed and fell straight to sleep.

Settled at our table with sample plates of all the good stuff: french toast, omelets, pancakes, and waffles, Porsche breaks the ice.

"Y'all fucked," she says, matter-of-factly.

Lily muffles her laugh with her hands, but she looks at me knowingly.

"Mind your damn business," I tell them, grinning.

"It is my business that you're walking differently today." Porsche laughs.

"I told you he was hung," Lily leans over and tells Porsche. "I could tell by how he walked. Where's he land on the dick-o-meter?" she asks.

We haven't brought out the dick-o-meter in a while. It goes Lil Smokie, hotdog, bun size dog, polish, and bulk shopping beef roll.

"I'm not sharing intimate details about my fiancé with you two!" I gasp and clutch my imaginary pearls.

"We deserve to know, dammit! We've been with you through it all. We've earned this," Porsche pleads.

I shake my head. Nope, I'm not giving that information. I'm not telling them a damn thing. This rendezvous was a one-off, and I'm holding it close.

"You suck. Cuz I know it was so damn good. I'm surprised you're not hoarse right now. I bet you were at it all night," Porsche says.

I cough and grin. She's not wrong.

I look at Lily, and she's giving me her puppy dog eyes.

Dru walks up to our table. Lily and Porsche crane their necks to look up at him. I burst out laughing, and so do they. Dru glances down at himself, making sure he remembered to zip his pants, then he looks up at us with a nervous smile. "What?" he asks.

"They're being ridiculous," I tell him. "Here, come sit by me. We have a little bit of everything. What do you want?" I offer.

Lily leans over to Porsche and whispers loud enough for everyone at the table to hear, "She's making his plate. It was that good."

I shoot daggers at Lily with my eyes. I can't believe she's doing me like this. I expect that kind of behavior from Porsche. Lily is kind and sweet and she has my back. Today, she's a traitor.

Dru chuckles and eats his eggs.

"How'd you spend your night last night, Black Bruce Wayne? Saving the people of Puerto Rico from danger?

"He was deep in the Bat Cave," Lily replies, snickering into her orange juice.

"Stop it!" I chastise them. "You two are doing too much."

Dru just laughs, unaffected by all of this chatter.

"What's on the agenda today?" I ask, trying to change the subject.

"I had a plan, but after this informative breakfast, I'm rethinking my ability to be with all three of you today," he says.

"No, we can be good. What's the plan?" Lily promises.

"I'm a man who loves to take his woman shopping," he begins.

"You're going to drag us along while she shops?" Porsche interrupts. "No offense, C."

I throw my hands in the air. "None taken."

"No, Porsche," he says, pointedly. "I'm going to take all three of you shopping. The plan is to spoil all three of you. She went on a spree yesterday." He turns to me and there's lust in his eyes that makes me blush.

Porsche is struck dumb. Her mouth is open, and for once in her life, she's silent.

"Are you serious?" Lily asks, her voice barely above a whisper.

"I am, and I know I need to tell you not to be shy. You'll be like Charisse and try to stay within a budget when I said she had no limits. Spend to your heart's content." He turns to Porsche. "You keep yourself under control. My card has no limit, but I know you'll be able to press it anyway." He winks at her, and she cracks a smile.

We spend the day shopping in a different area. Porsche behaves herself. She actually held back, liking the idea of balling out, but she wasn't actually able to do it. She did exactly what I did the day before: tried things on, wondered over shiny pieces, and walked the catwalk in sexy high-heeled shoes, but she bought very little. I kept my eyes on Dru the whole time. She'll be getting a nice delivery when she's back home. It may be there before she returns.

Spoiling me is one thing, but this man taking the time to spoil my friends put my feelings for him in a totally different category. If I wasn't already falling for him, I definitely am now.

On the plane at the end of our trip, Porsche and Lily sit in the row in front of us, exhausted and passed out. Dru sits in the seat next to me, lifting up the armrest between us and scooting close to me.

"So, how was your break?" he asks, a grin on his face. He twirls one of my curls around his finger.

I lean into him and sigh. "It was the best break I've had in all my years as a teacher. Thank you. We will never forget this."

He nods and nuzzles his face in my neck. "You're welcome," he whispers and brushes his lips against me.

I shiver and clench my fists at my side. He can't do this to me right now. A private jet is the perfect way to join the mile high club, but not with my girls right up there. Plus, my body is sore. Every night we slept in the bed was spent tangled up together. My lady parts need a break. It's been a long time since they got this kind of attention.

A part of me worries about what this means for when we're back home, and what it means for our agreement, but I'm afraid to bring it up. Everything has been too perfect this weekend, and I don't want to burst the bubble before we have to.

"I've never deplaned this quickly," Lily exclaims as she grabs her bag and walks off the plane.

Chance waits for us with the door open at the bottom of the stairs. "Did you enjoy your trip, ladies?" he asks as we step into the car.

"I can't even describe how wonderful it was, honestly," Porsche says. Chance nods.

"I'm happy to hear that," he says, closing the door behind the four of us.

"Dru, really, thank you so much for this weekend. It was the break I didn't know I needed. I won't be letting my kids out early at all this week. I'm gonna teach bell to bell," Porsche declares.

I guffaw. She's lying; she'll be letting them leave two minutes early by Wednesday. "Hush Charisse. I will."

"Okay, Friend. I believe you," I tell her.

Once Porsche and Lily are home, Dru sits close to me. "I had fun with you this weekend."

"Oh yeah?" I ask.

"You already know that."

I giggle. "Yes, I do. I know a lot more about you than I did four days ago," I tell him, raising my eyebrows.

"I know what you taste like," he says, making me clench my legs.

"Dru. What's this—"

He interrupts me. "No. I don't want to analyze. Let's just keep living, okay? I want to do whatever feels right with you in the moment. Can we do that instead?" His eyes plead with me.

I don't know exactly what that looks like or what it means, but I don't actually want to talk about it either, so I agree.

Chapter 25

Charisse

Puerto Rico was a week ago, my skin is still sun-kissed, and I'm still debuting new clothes at school. All of my free time is filled with wedding planning. It's all very meta. I'm stressed about planning my fake wedding. It's such a strange feeling. None of this is real, but the dress fitting next week will be real. The invitations I just ordered are real. The bouquet samples I've been sent are real.

Flipping through the bridal magazine on my couch at the end of my school day, my sister comes to my mind. I bet she's doing the same thing right now, so I send her a text.

Y: Hey! It's good to hear from you! Wedding planning is tough. Our budget went down for some reason, and I'm having to rethink everything I wanted.

Me: That's annoying. I'm sorry sis!

Y: It is what it is. I'm in love, so it doesn't really matter how, just as long as we make those vows.

My fingers hover over my phone, wanting to tell her what I know, but it's not the time. It's not my business, right? Instead, I find the video from my engagement and send it to her.

Me: Guess what!

A few minutes after I send her the video, she calls me.

"Oh my GAWD!" she screams into the phone. "He proposed? I'm so happy for you!" She's practically yelling at me, but it is genuine, and that nagging feeling ties my stomach up again. More joy for me based on a lie.

"Dru knows your fiancé," I blurt out. Fuck, why the fuck did I just say that? We're doing good, having a great conversation.

"Oh yeah, through business or something?" she asks, joy still in her voice.

"Or something..." I trail off.

"What?" she asks, confused.

"Your fiancé is dating the CFO of Dru's business," I whisper into the phone, shame already burning through my gut.

"What did you just say?" She grinds out through her teeth.

"Nique, Dru told me your fiancé has been dating the CFO of his business for months now. She has pictures of him all over her socials. And they're not the kind you can interpret as something else."

"Send it to me," she demands, suddenly monotone and cold.

I search the woman's name on socials and send Yanique the link. "I'm sorry," I say when the read bubbles light up on my end.

Yanique doesn't say anything else. She doesn't make a single sound. "Do you want me to come see you? Do you want to come stay with me for a while?" I offer.

"How long have you known?" Her voice is sharp, scary.

"Yanique—"

"HOW LONG HAVE YOU KNOWN?" She screams it at me.

"Since your engagement party," I confess, feeling like a piece of trash.

Silence meets me on the other end.

"Hello?" I look at the screen of my phone, and I'm no longer in a conversation with my sister. I send her an "I'm so sorry" text, then I call Dru.

"Hey," I say when he answers the phone.

"What's wrong?" he asks, alarm in his voice.

My heart skips a beat at how perceptive he is to a simple change in my tone. I take a shaky breath. "I told my sister."

"Damn, what'd she say?"

"She asked me how long I knew. When I told her, she hung up on me." My voice cracks, but I don't let myself cry. There was no right way to do this other than to just fucking tell her. These tears are hers to cry, not mine.

"You feel bad?" he asks so gently.

"I do," I begin, taking another shuddering breath in and exhaling slowly. "Not for telling her though or knowing for so long."

"You feel bad for your sister who's planning a real, dream wedding that just got her heart crushed," he says, speaking exactly what my heart feels.

"Yes. And she's going to blame me somehow. She's going to stay mad at me longer than she's mad at him," I whine.

"If that's her process, you gotta let her have it," he tells me. "You've done what you can. It's between them now. Are you all right?" I hear his keys jingle, and I know he's about to drive his actual car here. I don't want to interrupt his Saturday, but I could use his company right now.

"Not really," I admit. "Are you coming?" My voice wobbles. I'm not trying to be dramatic, but it's just coming out of me.

"Yes I am. You hungry?" he asks.

"Always." I manage a giggle.

"I'll be there in thirty minutes."

"Okay."

He arrives with ramen. Not the ten cent ramen from the grocery store, but the socials ramen with all kinds of meat and vegetables in it.

"I told them no eggs because I know how you hate breakfast foods in non-breakfast situations," he tells me, handing me my take-out container and a fork.

"You know exactly what to say to make me swoon. Thank you." I look up at him and smile.

"That I do!" He gets his food situated and finally sits down beside me. "Feeling better?"

"A little. I've just buried myself deeper into wedding planning. My brain keeps reminding me that she's marrying a cheater while you and I are cheating by getting married." I sigh.

"Don't think about it like that. We will be together for a long time. Nothing about maintaining our facade will be easy. We won't be cheating our way through this. We'll be working harder than most people have to in order to keep it all going."

He's right. Faking our marriage for almost two years will be harder than people who love each other trying to maintain a marriage. I nod and slurp my noodles. He sits up straighter and looks me dead in the eye.

"Stop it and let me eat, damn!" I slap him on his shoulder.

"We can be rough with it if you want," he says, attempting to swipe everything off my table.

"You better stop! I'm hungry, and if you plan on wearing me out tonight, I need my nutrients. We seriously need to plan this wedding though," I tell him.

"We can hire someone to do that, you know. You shouldn't have to put all this work into your fake wedding. Save it for your real one," he tells me.

My real wedding. I laugh. My youth is dwindling away. By the time our marriage is over, I'll be in my midthirties. Who's getting married in their midthirties? My mom's already bugging me now.

"Oh shit! I haven't told my parents." I jump up from my seat and start pacing. "Do I send the video? Or a text? Do I call?"

There's two more people I have to lie to. Damn, this sounded so great when I made the deal with Dru, but now it feels disgusting. Being with him obviously isn't awful, but how often this feeling of guilt stabs me in my gut is becoming unbearable.

"Do you think we should call this whole thing off?" I ask him, chewing on my nails.

"No."

"Why not?" I whine.

"Because you may have paid off your loans and gotten what you needed out of this, but it would end up hurting me. I'd be back at square one." He crosses his arms and leans back in his chair.

I roll my eyes. "Do you need your mom's company? Aren't you rich enough?"

His gaze is neutral. "Yes, I'm rich enough. And you know that's not why I want the company. You know, because I've told you before, that it's my family's legacy, and it needs to come into the twenty-first century," he tells me through clenched teeth.

I stop pacing and whirl on him. "Shouldn't you find a woman for real then? You're cheating. And you're paying me, pimping me around, to deceive your family. It feels gross." I put my hands on my hips and glare at him.

He turns fully in his chair to face me, and he stares me down with an intensity I've never seen before. His eyes are narrowed, and his lips form a straight line. I can tell he's choosing his words, and that he's meticulously thinking through his next statement. My heart pounds out of my chest as I wait.

"First of all, you are under contract. As anxious as I was to get under contract, I did make sure that the contract was airtight. So you will owe me so much money if you fuck this up. Second, just because you've gotten the money that you need and now your morals are suddenly kicking in doesn't mean that my reward will not come to me. So this wedding is on. This marriage is happening. We can like each other while we do this, or we can hate each other. It's your choice, but it is happening."

I stand in front of him, dumbfounded, and realizing that I am stuck, and we shouldn't have slept together because everything is much more complicated now. And I don't know how to act anymore. While I am wildly attracted to him, and the sex is amazing, this isn't a real relationship. I'm being paid to be with him. I'm hoeing myself out, and now he's going to hold me to it like the businessman that he is.

I turn away before the tears can well up in my eyes. "I understand," I whisper, not daring to face him again. "You should probably head home now. And I think it'll be a good idea to hire a wedding planner. She can do whatever she wants, plan her dream wedding. Just tell me when and where to show up." I walk into my bedroom and close the door.

Chapter 26

Dru

It's been a week since I blew up on Charisse in her apartment, and we still haven't spoken. Neither of us has called or texted the other. I'm giving her space to sort through her feelings, even though I play my little speech over and over again in my head. I lawyered her. I pulled the only lever I have with her, and it was the wrong thing to do. She's more than a business transaction to me, but I told her that's exactly what she is. She's my means to an end.

The moment I finished talking, I knew I'd gone too far. Her eyes got glossy, and she turned away from me to hide how much I'd hurt her. And I'd stood my ground like a barbarian. I'm in my office, running it through my mind again and again when my phone rings.

"Hey, Mom!" I throw my good cheer voice on.

"Dru, baby love, how are you doing?" she asks.

"I'm doing all right?" Mom never calls to just see how I'm doing. Something's up.

"You don't sound so sure." She ventures.

"No, I'm fine. Just reading a memo. What's up?"

"I want to have a family dinner with your fiancé. She's so beautiful, Dru. I'm so happy for you," she gushes.

"Yeah, I know, Mom. When?"

"Tomorrow night."

Shit. I have to call her, make up with her, and convince her to go to family dinner today. It's not going to go well.

"Ok, Mom. We'll be there."

"I love you baby child."

"I love you too, Mom."

I text Charisse when we hang up, but it's the middle of her fourth period, and I know that class works her nerves so much. She has to give them her full attention. I pull my jacket off the back of my chair and rush out.

Chance drops me off in front of Charisse's school, and I realize I have no idea what I'm doing or what I'm going to say. Hell, I don't even know if they'll let me in.

I walk into the office, and the first person I see is Porsche. I have some luck. Damn.

"What are you doing here, Scrooge McDuck?" she asks with a sneer.

"That's the strangest insult I've ever heard," I tell her, laughing.

"Don't laugh, Richy Rich. I'm just getting started. Why are you here?" She crosses her arms over her chest and leans her weight on to one leg.

"I need to talk to Charisse," I say.

"Is this the fiancé?" An older lady asks from behind the desk, a smile blooming on her face.

"The one and only," I say, flashing my brightest smile and straightening out my jacket lapels.

"She's in room 205, upstairs and to the left. Are you here to surprise her?" she gushes.

"Something like that."She's not completely wrong. My showing up will be a surprise.

"I'll show him," Porsche tells the lady before she turns to me with a scowl on her face. She walks quickly out of the office, and I follow her closely. So close that when she abruptly stops at the bottom of the stairs, I bump right into her.

"Look, your money don't mean shit to me. You can have back everything you paid for, and I wouldn't give a damn. The way you hurt my girl. The things you said to her. Dude, that was unnecessary and harsh, and I'll do what I need to do to hurt you if you do it again." Porsche steps so close to me I can smell the gum she's chewing. "Her classroom is upstairs on the left. I'm only letting you pass because I can see how you really feel for her written all over your face. Don't fuck with her like that again."

I nod, needing to get away from her as quickly as possible, and run up the stairs. I take the stairs two at a time, racing but not sure why I'm moving so fast. She's not going anywhere, and I don't really know what I'm going to say. I need to see her. That's what it is; I need to see her. When I reach her door, I hold the door handle for far too long, trying to determine my purpose here. The door is yanked out of my hand, and a young girl stares up at me with her eyes wide.

"Miss Turner, I think your man is here. He's fine." The girl giggles and gives me a full up and down before leaving the classroom. I frown. That's not what I needed today at all. I don't want to have to add myself to any registry over some young girl oogling over me. I shake my hands out, needing to cleanse this whole situation.

"Dru, what are you doing here?" She comes out of her classroom and closes the door slightly.

"I. Family di—I. I'm sorry," I finally decide to say. "Shit, I'm sorry for everything I said last week. You didn't deserve that, and you have to know you mean more to me than a business. I got scared that you'd ruin the plan, and I freaked out.

"Why are you here right now?"she asks, not buying anything I just said.

"My mom invited you to our family dinner," I say, resigned. There's no need to lie. I'm here because I need her to go to a family dinner. That's it. Sure I screwed everything up with what I said, but whether she likes me or not, I need something from her right now.

"I'll pay you to go," I plead. After it leaves my mouth, I feel like an ass.

"You'll what?" she whispers, closing the classroom door completely and taking the stance that I know means that she's pissed off.

"Shit. I'm messing this all up. My mom just wants to have dinner as a family with my fiancée. and you're my fiancée."

"You interrupted my job to offer to pay me to whore myself out to your family more? You came up to my place of business, and you are asking me for a favor?" She looks at me like I'm the most disappointing human being on the planet. "I don't believe this is a part of my contract. Family dinners aren't included in the contract. I read it after I signed it, but I did read it. There were no stipulations like this. So no, I won't be going to your little family dinner. Figure something else out." She opens her classroom door steps inside, and closes the door in my face.

It feels like a walk of shame as I go back down the stairs, and stand outside the school waiting for Chance to pick me up. I sit in the back of the car with my head in my hands, lost. I don't know what to tell my mom and dad and sister and brothers. What's a good excuse for my fiancée to miss the first family dinner she's been invited to? How am I going to fix this with her and with my family?

Chance drops me off at my studio; I need to work some things out in my head. I find a 2x4 laying on the ground, and I pick up some nails in my hammer. I set each nail in the wood standing up, and then I pound them all into the 2x4 with all of my strength. The hammer hits the nail on the head every time ten times in a row, and it feels good to get this frustration out. I'm no closer to having a solution, but I don't feel as angry anymore.

I'll skip the family dinner, and I'll say we're both sick. That's an easy solution for my family, but I still don't have a solution for Charisse. She still hates me, and we haven't even walked down the aisle yet.

My sister video calls me right after I text my mom to tell her that we can't make it because we're sick.

"Why are you lying to your mother like that?" she accuses me.

"What are you talking about?"

"You know what the hell I'm talking about. You're lying about being sick. You did something to screw this up, didn't you?"

"Damn it, why do you know everything?"

"Because I'm the big sister, and you're the idiot baby brother. Of course you did something to screw up the stupid thing that you already did. What are you going to do to fix it?"

"Hell if I know."

"So you're just going to let her go? You're going to force her into this fake relationship, and you're going to make her hate you for however long you have her under contract. That's really shitty, by the way. I'd hate hearing the word contract."

"I don't know what I'm going to do. I kind of want to just run away from all of it. I want to just have it all disappear or go back in time and never do this in the first place. This was stupid, and she's right. I'm cheating."

"But you have feelings for her, don't you?"

"Of course I do, but what am I going to do about that now? I really fucked up. I don't think she's going to just take me back and let the deal play out." I resign. It's over. Our jovial relationship, everything we were building is over.

"What if she's actually the one?" my sister asks.

I consider it. I hadn't thought about that. I'd just been enjoying her company. Our romps in Puerto Rico flash in my mind.

"Ugh, you had sex with her too? Dru, you're disgusting. Either have this be a business deal or a relationship. You've blurred the lines too much."

"Is there a marquee scrolling my every thought? I can't keep talking to you. Apparently you can just see all my deepest, darkest secrets."

"You're deflecting," she says, calling me out. "Stop shitting where you eat. Stop screwing the help."

"The help?" I look at her, incredulous.

"She's doing a service for you. You're paying her for it. She's the help."

"That's a big overgeneralization."

"And it's true," she declares.

"Shit, yeah it is." I sigh.

"So, the real deal is that you need to figure out what she's going to be for you because she can't be both."

I end the call with a lot on my mind.

Chapter 27

Charisse

"Porsche," I stand in her classroom with my hands on my hips.

"What'd he have to say? Did he apologize?" Pride beams from her. "I told him off before I took him up to your room."

"You brought him to my classroom?" I scowl at her.

"Yeah, and I told him not to fuck with you anymore." She crosses her arms and leans against her desk.

"No. He requested my presence at his family dinner tomorrow."

"Did he lead with that?" she asks.

"Yeah, just jumped right into it. A disingenuous apology, not even much of an intro. He just asked me to go to his family dinner tomorrow," I told her.

"That motherfucker!" Porsche yells.

That's exactly what I called him in my head. I don't know how to resolve this, but I can't fake it for an intimate family dinner.

"What are you going to do?" Porsche asks me, concern riddled in her eyes.

"I'm not going to the family dinner, but I'm under contract, and I've already been paid. I can manage to survive throughout the rest of this contract to get my money. So I'm going to be miserable for the next almost two years, but I'm also going to be paid. I'm willing to sacrifice the time for the money," I confess.

"Two years? You can fake a marriage and everything that you have to put on for that long? It was cool when you two were getting along, and when I knew that you two would fall in love and just ended up actually married for real, but close to two years of just hating every moment doesn't seem like it's worth the money," she tells me.

While she might be right, I don't have a choice. I know that contract is rock solid. It's a brick wall that nothing can permeate, so unless I want to owe him money, I have to follow through.

"How hard can it be to just go through the motions when people are watching? I can show up to a charity ball or to a dinner or any other event in a beautiful dress with a beautiful smile on my face."

"It sounds like that on paper," she begins. "But I'm sure it's going to be much more than that, and it's going to eat your soul."

"I'm under contract," I remind her. "I don't have a choice."

At home, I look into my fully stocked fridge and find a way to be grateful for this contract. I don't get paid for another four days, and at this point last month, the fridge would be empty, and I'd be eating noodles.

I make myself a simple chicken Alfredo dish and sit down to lesson plan while I eat. It's the time of year where I start getting my seniors ready for the real world by making them do projects where they have to plan a real life. We read the play, *A Raisin in the Sun*, and do a real life project on how they would spend the $10,000 of insurance money,except I change it due to inflation and make it $200,000. They decide if they want to buy a house, enroll in college, or start a business. I assign them different states; they choose the city and everything else, but they have to decide and budget and plan what they can afford to do.

Maybe I need to do that myself. I have $200,000 in my account right now. I need to be thinking about my future and what I want to do after my two-year sentence is up.

I'm creating groups for the students to work in and randomly assigning states when my phone dings.

Dru: Are you busy?

I'm not sure how to answer that. I'm kind of busy, but not busy enough to not be able to text. He asked which is an effort, but do I really want to talk to him?

Me: Not really, what's up?

Dru: I'm sorry about earlier. That was very selfish of me. We are already in a tough spot, and my approach did nothing to improve it.

Me: I appreciate your apology.

Dru: I'm also sorry for my outburst. While my reasons for this deal are important to me, I didn't have to talk to you like that. I could have been civil and explained myself better.

Me: Thank you.

I wait for him to tell me we can call the whole thing off, but he doesn't text me again, so I get back to lesson planning.

I've settled back into my life routine by the time Wednesday rolls around and it's time for me and my girls to have our weekly dinner date.They don't know, but I'm paying. I won't be telling Porsche until after she's ordered, so she doesn't try to ball out on my budget.

This is the first time in a month or so that we actually have to drive ourselves to this meal. It's also the first time in a month or so that the meal is not completely paid for by Dru. I'm only upset about the driving because I would love to get drunk tonight.

"You look nice," Lily tells me when I knock on her door.

"Thanks, I feel nice today. It's the first time in a while that I haven't felt like trash."

She nods, knowingly, but she doesn't press me to explain. I haven't wanted to talk about anything relating to Dru all week. Thankfully, both of my girls have respected that.

Porsche arrives a few minutes after me, and we rock paper scissors to see who's going to drive thus being our designated driver.

"Dammit! I wanted to drink!" Porsche whines when she loses the final round. I sigh in relief, because I'm drinking tonight.

I plug in the directions to a restaurant we've never been to before. It's usually too rich for our blood, but it wasn't rich enough for Dru to have ever sent us: a nice middle ground.

"How are you doing?" Porsche asks as she drives, looking up at me through the rearview mirror.

"I'm doing," I tell her, and it's 100 percent true. I'm just existing and trying not to think about my impending nuptials.

"Have you heard from him?" Lily asks.

"I just got an updated timeline. You should be receiving invitations to our engagement party by the end of this week, and the party is next weekend. I texted my parents and told them I was engaged, but they're too wrapped up in Yanique's drama to really care that much, which is actually a relief. Now we'll see if they all show up to this engagement party."

"Damn," Porsche says. "That's a lot of drama in one location. Do you think your sister is going to bring her fiancé to your engagement party? Are you going to see Dru ahead of time?"

"I don't know. I just know that I have a dress fitting this weekend that you two are going to, and the rest will come out in the wash. My parents will either RSVP or they won't. Same for my sister. I'll just have to see. What I do know is that I have to be there, so I will."

"How long can you keep this up?" Lily asks as we pull into a parking spot at the restaurant.

"I believe I can keep this up for twenty months," I tell her.

"If you say so."

Once we're seated and have our drinks delivered to us—a nice bubbly soda for Porscha that she pouts at—we get down to it.

"Ok, we really need to talk, Charisse," Lily says before I take my first sip.

I knew this was coming, but I don't want to talk about anything.

"What about?" I feign ignorance.

"About your life crumbling before us. Your family isn't talking to you. Your mom reached out to me," Porsche tells me.

My mom talked to Porsche? About what? Why? The questions roll around in my head, but none come out of my mouth. Instead, I stare at her with my mouth wide open.

"About the lie you told your sister," she tells me, raising her eyebrows.

"Are you serious?" I ask. I take a deep breath and chug my frozen margarita. Then I slam my hand on the table as brain freeze paralyzes my thoughts.

"Yes, her fiancé told her those pictures were old, and she was reposting them to cause trouble," Porsche explains. "So, they're all pissed about that. And about your engagement announcement being in text form."

The betrayal in all of this feels like a hot knife going through my heart. My mother expressed more to my friend than she's expressed to me (good or bad) in the past five years.

"What did you say?" I ask, hoping she defended me.

"I said you were looking out for your sister and had no way of knowing the pictures were old—even though I know that's bullshit. You know I'm not about to argue with your mother. I also told her you didn't want to make a big fuss about your engagement in light of what's going on with your sister. I tried my best to have your back, but you know how your people are. That was yesterday, and I waited until today, so I could tell you in person, over a drink I wish I had right now."

A rush of relief washes over me. At least these girls have my back. I can always depend on that one fact.

Chapter 28

Charisse

Chance stands on the other side of my door. I haven't seen him since I last saw Dru which was over two weeks ago. I'm not sure if I'll see Dru at all, but I know Porsche and Lily will be there. That knowledge plus champagne will get me through this day.

"Miss Charisse, it's good to see you," Chance says cheerily after I open the door.

"It's good to see you too," I reply, feeling more comfortable in his presence. Something about him disarms and calms me.

He holds my door, and I hold my breath wondering if Dru will be inside. I step into the empty vehicle, and audibly exhale.

"I miss this treatment," Porsche says as she gets in.

"I do too," I admit. I was getting used to having a driver and all the perks of being with Dru. I find myself missing Dru more though. As much as I hate to admit it.

Lily pops into the car, an orange ray of sunshine. "This is the life we deserve. We have to find a way to become independently wealthy."

"Damn right," I say.

Our car ride is long, so Lily tells us about the paint and sip Dru scheduled for everyone at Fresh Flavor Fix.

"He asked me to design a logo for his company. The sale fell through, and he wants to do a rebranding. I'm pretty excited about it, and about how much he's paying me," she tells us.

"That's great!" I tell her, genuinely excited for her. She's been trying to break into graphic design, and this is a huge opportunity.

"I know. I didn't think you'd feel any way about it. I'm happy you're okay with it."

"No matter what I'm going through with Dru, I'd never mess up your bag." I lean into her.

We settle into easy conversation. Porsche has a new man, and she gushes over him.

"He's not balling like our boy Dru, but he's got a little something-something, and he's actually a good guy." She smiles wide, showing all her teeth, so I know she's really happy.

"I'm happy for you. How long have you been seeing him?" I ask.

"Since Puerto Rico. It was the break I needed to put me in an open state of mind. I leaned in to Dru's idea that I deserve this kind of treatment, and that I deserve someone who will shower me with the affection I need. I guess I did some of your manifesting, Lily," Porsche says, laughing.

Lily's cheesing and so am I. I love moments like this where we can just be genuinely happy for each other. If only I had something to be happy about.

"The last time I was dress shopping for an event with him, he flew me to New York. That would be nice, but I don't think we're in quite the same spot as we were," I confess. I pour a drink, hoping to drown the sadness that threatens to show its face.

Lily and Porsche stare at me, pity showing in their eyes.

"Stop looking at me like that," I demand, frowning and crossing my arms over my chest.

"Stop looking like that then," Porsche replies.

"Looking like what?"

"Like the love of your life broke your heart," Lily answers without skipping a beat.

The love of my life? Unlikely. The love of right now, maybe. I attempt a smile, but I just can't pull it off. Love of my life or love of right now makes no difference; I lost him and the easy fun we had together.

After an hour and a half, we arrive at a very chic gown shop. Chance opens the door for us, and we pile out of the car. A sharply dressed woman with a razor-sharp bob greets us.

"Charisse? The future Mrs. Dru Martin?" she asks.

I pause for half a second before I realize what persona I need to put on and smile. "The one and only," I say with a flourish of my left hand to show off the diamond engagement ring.

"We are so excited to find you the perfect engagement party dress...and hopefully your wedding dress too. I know Dru has impeccable taste. You must as well to be marrying him. I see you dressed down today though," she says with a wave of her hand at my outfit.

I want to melt into the floor and flow into the sewer grate. I didn't realize I was being judged today. There wasn't a memo about dressing up to dress shop. Out of the corner of my eye, I see Lily pull Porsche back.

"I'm going for the full Cinderella transformation," I reply, holding my head up high.

"Well, I'm Janay, and I'll be helping you transform." She does a dramatic twist on her toes and heads into the shop. "Please follow me."

"She's got a lot to say for a bitch whose lace can be seen from space," Porsche mutters.

"She's jealous that Charisse is the one shopping, and she's stuck selling the dresses. Don't feed off her energy," Lily says as she enters the shop first.

"Dru asked me to show you a couple of Annika DuBois dresses we have. So I've pulled them," Janay says as she continues her odd twirling around the shop.

"Is that the designer he flew you out to be fitted for the dress for the charity ball where he proposed?" Porsche loudly asks.

"No, that was Isolde Orion. I believe her dresses are exclusive. She doesn't sell them in shops; you have to fly out to her to be fitted or get something custom," I tell her. That dress was gorgeous.

"You think he's going to take you to her again?" Lily ponders as she peruses the dresses on the rack.

"Knowing Dru, that'll end up being a trip to Paris to have the dress custom designed and fitted exactly to her body," Porsche suggests.

I laugh at this narrative they're creating. It's not too far from the truth though. I wouldn't put it past him to have my wedding dress custom made. And I wouldn't hate it.

I grab the first dress off the rack. "Where do I try this on?" I ask Janay. She Vanna White presents the dressing room to me. I stifle a laugh. "Thanks."

I take my time removing my dressed down outfit, keeping my grumbling to myself. Janay's probably right outside the door waiting awkwardly for me to come out. As I stand in my underwear, my phone dings.

"Ugh, just give me a few minutes." I sigh, thinking it's my girls being impatient.

Dru: Has Janay insulted you yet?

Me: Lol. Immediately, before I even walked in. What's her deal?

Dru: She's crazy, but Annika likes her. She was busy this weekend, so we couldn't do a private fitting.

Me: I'm disappointed there wasn't a plane ride involved with this dress shopping.

Dru: Do you care about the environment at all?

Me: My one trip on a jet isn't going to be the straw that breaks the camel's back.

Dru: That's what everyone says.

Me: Why aren't you here?

My heart races after I press send. I shouldn't have asked him that. I need to leave good enough alone.

Dru: I didn't think you wanted me there.

Me: I didn't either, but now I do.

What am I doing?

Dru: I can make that happen.

Me: Really? Gonna hop on the PJ for a 15 minute flight?

Dru: I'm up the street. I had business here yesterday, and I wanted to handpick the dresses for you to try on. Will Porsche and Lily mind? Have you been dogging me to them all day?

Me: No. And no. What kind of fiancée do you think I am?

Dru: The fakest of the fake.

I change into the first dress. It's a strapless mermaid cut that says wedding dress more than engagement. Seeing myself in it makes me smile though. It's definitely a flattering cut on me. I might need a mermaid cut for the wedding.

"Are you ready for this?" I call out.

Porsch and Lily clap and cheer.

"No, you're not ready for this, but I'm coming out anyway." I laugh. I bounce out of the dressing room and back it up as I get to where I'm supposed to stand on and be ogled at. I shake my ass and do a little twerk in the dress. Porsche and Lily are squealing and clapping for me. I finally stop and stand up like a lady, and sitting front and center flanked by my best friends is Dru.

"It passes the twerk test," Dru says with a salacious grin on his face. I want to cover my body with my hands from the way he's looking at me. Porsche and Lily notice too, but they just look from him to me and back again with goofy grins on their faces.

"It sure does," I say, beaming—happy he's here. "What do you two think?" I ask Porsche and Lily. I do a model walk and twirl a few times.

"It fits that ass just right," Porsche says.

Dru fist bumps her, cosigning on what she said.

"It's beautiful, but I don't think it's an engagement dress. I've never been to a bougie engagement party, but those dresses are usually shorter, like a cocktail dress." She turns to Dru. "Is this a black tie affair?"

"Judging by my mom and sister's dresses, yes it is very much a formal, black-tie affair," he says to her.

"Ah hell! I need to buy something too," Porsche says.

"Janay, take their measurements and find them dresses too. Put it all on the card you have on file." He turns to Lily and Porsche. "Buy what you feel the most beautiful in. Don't worry about the cost." He winks at Porsche, knowing she's headed for the most expensive dress in her size, and he furrows his brows at Lily. She rolls her eyes and puts up her scout's honor fingers.

Janay looks exasperated. "Annika won't be happy to hear about any untoward treatment of my fiancé and her friends. Especially since we'll probably be buying two of her dresses from you today."

Janay flashes a fake smile and puts some pep in her step as

she assesses my friends' sizes visually and scampers off to pull dresses for them.

While the three of them search for dresses in the back of the shop, Dru approaches the stage I'm on and gazes up at me. His eyes tell me he wants to devour me. "I don't want to say or do anything to mess today up for you or your friends. You look ravishing in that dress. Buy it, regardless of if you wear it for the party or not. It was made for you."

I stare at him.

He runs his hand down his face and sighs, putting his hands in his pockets. "I want to talk to you. Can we have dinner tonight at my hotel? I'll have Porsche and Lily driven back when you're done here, if that's okay. I just need to talk to you."

I nod at him, and his face brightens. His words at my school cross my mind, and my heart hurts. I'm not going to hold a grudge though, and I will hear him out.

He leaves me and my friends to pick out our dresses. They could not be more different. Lily's is a coral color that pops on her skin. It's a spaghetti strapped dress with a cinched waist and a slip all the way up her leg. Porsche's dress of choice is a black, sequined number with capped sleeves and a deep u neckline that shows off her cleavage. The party is for a fake engagement, but there will be some real women there looking hot as hell.

Chapter 29

Charisse

I see my friends off before I go to where Dru is parked and let myself into the passenger door.

"Are you hungry?" he asks.

"Yes, I'm starving. Are there any ramen places nearby?" I've been craving some real ramen lately.

"The hotel I'm in has great ramen. Do you want to try that?" He sounds nervous, like we're on a first date and he's terrified of screwing it up.

"Yeah, let's do that."

We drive the short distance in silence before I ask, "Did you really have business here?"

"Yes. Yesterday. I stayed an extra night hoping you'd want to see me." He steals a glance in my direction.

"A minor risk that paid off handsomely. You're a good businessman." I laugh.

"I'm a good gambler is more like it."

He parks the car, and we walk into the hotel lobby. It's grandiose, with sky high ceilings and chandeliers. We walk side by side to the restaurant tucked in the back, our bodies centimeters apart.

"Mr. Martin, it's nice to see you here this evening," the hostess says. "I have a private table for you. Right this way."

"Did you call ahead?" I ask.

He shakes his head.

"Richie Rich perk, eh?"

He smiles at me and follows the hostess.

"I'm sorry," he tells me before we order drinks.

The waitress appears the instant it leaves his lips.

"I'll have bottled water, and my date will have a frozen strawberry margarita and cup of water with light ice and no lemon." He doesn't hesitate at all to order for me, and I have nothing to say because he's spot on.

"You said some pretty shitty things," I tell him, needing to get it off my chest.

"I know." He sighs, making eye contact with me. "I don't have an excuse. There was no reason for that. I was an asshole to you, and I don't deserve to be at this table dining with you. So thank you for coming."

I don't know what made me come. Or what compelled me to ask him to the dress shop, other than I just miss him: asshole or not.

"How'd the family dinner go?"

"I didn't go either. I already told them you were sick. It would have been a bad move to leave you home sick. And in doing that, I understood your perspective. All of this lying is exhausting," he confesses.

I nod. "It makes you feel heavy and disgusting."

"It does. I'm sorry I got you wrapped up in it," he says softly.

"You didn't force my hand, Dru. I signed that contract the same day I got it without having any legal counsel look it over. I jumped in head first, and I didn't like when you called me into the part of the game I wasn't ready for. We are both at fault here."

I can see his body relax and loosen up.

"You did get all money-man on me though. It wasn't attractive at all."

"I did. I keep replaying the whole scene in my head, and I want to punch myself in the mouth. I'm embarrassed about the whole thing," he tells me. He reaches for my hand and kisses it.

"I'm so sorry, Charisse. I've missed you so much. Do you accept my apology?" he pleads with me.

He looks tortured, like his happiness depends on what I say. I sit back and cross my arms over my chest, acting like I'm thinking it over. Dru gets antsy in his seat—adjusting the silverware, folding and unfolding his napkin.

"I forgive you, Dru, but don't ever pull that shit on me again."

He jumps out of his seat and kisses me. It's not a peck on the cheek either. It's a deep, passionate kiss where I can taste the lemon from his water and his blood alcohol level just rose from the margarita I've been drinking. When our mouths finally part, he grips the back of my neck and rests his forehead on mine. "I did find my dream girl and hired her to marry me." He sighs before he sits back down.

Back at my apartment after a nice dinner and drive home with Dru, what he said about his dream girl replays in my head. Was he just being dramatic, or did he really mean it?

My phone rings while I'm undressing for the shower. It's Yanique. My pulse races, and I take a shaky, deep breath before I answer it.

"Yanique, how are you?" I try to sound excited to hear from her.

"I'm good, sis. How about you? I heard you and your man had a falling out," she hints with a weird tone.

I want to act surprised, but there are cameras everywhere, so I tell the truth. "Yeah, we did. A big one. I was ready to cancel everything."

"Oh, sis, what happened?" she asks, the fake concern in her voice makes my teeth hurt.

"We had a disagreement about something fundamental to our relationship." I keep it vague. It's not any of her business: real or fake.

"Aw, so there's only going to be one wedding this year then?" she asks with a brightness in her voice.

"Oh, you canceled yours?" I ask, fighting back now and playing the same game she is.

"Wha- No! Your information was false. They dated before, and when she found out we were together, she reposted those pictures. He's 100 percent dedicated to me," she proclaims.

I roll my eyes, but I keep the charade going. "Wonderful! I'm sorry I gave you misinformation. I was trying to protect you."

"I understand."

"I'm still getting married though. My engagement party is next week. You got the invitation, right? I gave the planner your address. We haven't spoken about the RSVPs yet although, we'll have a seat for you and your fiancé whether you RSVP or not. It's black tie, so wear a gown, okay?"

She huffs and mumbles about having to get off the phone. I don't like playing her games, but she's not going to get the best of me. My heart hurts though. She's still my sister, and both of us will be getting divorced at some point.

My mom has called me a few times since I sent the engagement video. I haven't been able to deal with what I know she's going to say, so I've ignored all the calls. Talking to Yanique gave me the boost I needed to just get it over with and face my mom, so I call her.

"Hey baby!" she exclaims when she answers the phone.

I'm already thrown off by her tone.

"Hey Mom, how's it going?"

"It's busy. Your sister's wedding planning takes up so much time. She dragged me dress shopping for a whole weekend, making me sit through her trying on a hundred dresses." She laughs.

The sting of them doing this without me hurts, but why should I expect anything different?

"Did she pick one?" I ask.

"Yeah, it's gorgeous. Lots of lace and sparkle. She looks like a princess," she tells me with pride in her voice.

"That's great! I found my engagement party dress today. Porsche and Lily helped me pick it out."

"Uh huh," she says, distracted. I hear the news in the background.

"Okay, well, I just wanted to say hi. I'll let you—oh, did you rsvp to my engagement party? It's next weekend."

"Yeah, yeah, I got it," she says. "I'll talk to you later, Risse. Love you."

The call disconnects, and I hold the phone in my hand feeling like I've just been hit by a train. Why did I feel bad about lying to them? They think this whole thing is real, and they still don't care. The proximity to my sister's wedding is close, but there's enough time in between to be able to enjoy both.

I'll always be insignificant to them. I don't know why I bother caring about either one of them at all.

Chapter 30

Dru

Everything is where it's supposed to be. My haircut is on point. My tuxedo is immaculate. The box I meticulously wrapped myself sits in the front seat with Chance. I'm ready for tonight.

"Let's hit it," I tell Chance from the back of the car. He pulls off and heads to Charisse's apartment.

Leslie and I have been planning this party nonstop for two weeks. The decor is sophisticated and as upscale as it gets. The color scheme is black and silver. Everyone was instructed to wear those colors, except for Charisse. Janay let me know she picked a red dress, so her red and my red will stand out. Janay also let me know that Lily picked a coral dress, so I had to request the same dress be made in silver for her. It was finished and delivered to her yesterday.

I don't know how anyone does this without a wedding planner or with limited funds. This isn't even the wedding, but the planning and constant changes are nerve-wracking. Charisse doesn't know it, but she'd be happy to have had no hand in this. All of the work would have driven her mad.

I hope she enjoys herself tonight. It's a bittersweet night, and I plan to do my best to enjoy every moment of it. Her mother and sister declined the invitation. I asked her friends if I should let her know, and they were split. Porsche said to tell her beforehand to not have the evening ruined. Lily said to let her figure it out on her own, so she's not upset the whole time leading up. I hope to have her so happy and distracted that she doesn't notice, so I took Lily's advice.

I step out of the car and walk to Charisse's door. My nerves suddenly kick in, and I have to take a deep breath before I knock. I requested that she get ready alone. I didn't want her distracted or out of her mindset before I picked her up. Tonight needs to go well; it's very important.

She opens the door on my first knock, and if she isn't the most perfect woman on Earth, I don't know who else could be. I put my hand on my heart and step back to get a full view of her.

The dress is cherry red. It's a one shoulder gown with a fitted bodice that accentuates that tiny waist of hers. The waist has silver accents. The skirt flows out, and the slit on the side makes me want to slide my hand all the way up her leg.

"Damn!" is all I can manage to say. Her red lips beg me to kiss them. Her flawless face is just made better by the make-up she's wearing. It's just enough to accentuate all of her beauty. She's stunning.

"Oh yeah?" she says, twirling for me and sticking that leg out of the slit.

"You trying to cause problems tonight?" I ask, moving in close to her and putting an arm around her waist. I give her a peck on her cheek and push down the thought of doing more to her.

"I'm trying to go to this party and put myself on display." She sighs.

"You'll be the center of attention for sure," I tell her as I help her into the car.

"Miss Charisse, you are stunning today," Chance says to her from the front of the car.

"Back off my girl, Chance!" I say with a smile.

He throws his hands in the air and looks at me from the rearview mirror. "Ready to go Boss?"

I nod, and we head off.

"I want you to not worry about anything or anyone tonight. Don't even act like it's an engagement party, just have fun, okay? I've got all of your favorite songs on deck. So just dance the night away. I have a few scheduled kisses. We can skip them if you want to. The cue will be a wink. Wink back if you're not feeling it. We'll give speeches at the end of the night. I wrote yours— it's delightful and full of flattery about me. You'll go first, then I have a surprise for you." I've slipped into my planning mode. My nerves make me do that, but it feels better to have a plan for things.

"Sounds good!" she says, staring out the window.

I shoot a text to the DJ to let him know we're arriving and to start the playlist. Porsche told me that if I play this song, she can't help but to dance, so I want it playing the moment we enter.

I help her out of the car, and we hold hands and walk in. Our first step into the ballroom is met by bass thumping. Charisse drops my hands and kneels down a bit and throws her hands in the air. I scan the room for Porsche. Porsche gives me a knowing nod when I spot her, and I bow to her in thanks.

Her friends surround her, and she dances hard for a solid thirty minutes. I stand off to the side, watching her and bouncing to the music. This playlist is fire.

"You're up to something," my sister says as she approaches.

"You look great, Dreya!" I tell her. She's been stressed about losing her baby weight. I'm not focused on that though. There's joy in her face that I haven't seen in a while. "Is my niece finally letting you sleep?" I ask.

"A full six hours baby!" she yells and pumps her fist in the air.

I smile at her.

"Showering me with true compliments won't deter me from figuring out what you're up to." She puts her hands on her hips and glares at me.

"All in due time, Dreya. Go enjoy a baby-free night," I tell her.

I don't want any distractions. The music is about to slow down, and we have a slow dance and a kiss coming up. I down my drink and wait for the last few notes of the song to finish. Then I make my way onto the dance floor and take Charisse's hand.

"May I have this dance?" I ask her. The slow song's first few chords play.

Charisse smiles, looking into my eyes. I briefly wonder what she's searching for, then I pull her close, wrapping my arms around her waist, and we sway to the music.

"Are you having fun?" I ask her. She's sweating, and her hairs tousled. Of course she's having fun.

"The time of my life. It's like prom, but with my best friends here. This place is beautiful. I love the silver and black and how everyone matches it. You coordinated all of that, didn't you?" she asks, a big smile on her face.

I nod and pull her closer to me. I love talking to her, but I just want to be here with her right now. I press my face into hers, and she leans into me. I take one hand off her waist and hold her hand with it, bringing it to my mouth and kissing it.

"Is that the kiss? I think the people want more than that." She laughs, then leans forward and kisses me softly. I part my lips and take her lip into my mouth. She moans and presses into me more. I let her hand go and slide my hand up her neck, planting small kisses on her lips. She sighs into my mouth, and as much as I want to keep going, I begin to pull back. I can't forget we're on the dance floor in front of a whole crowd of people.

The song ends just in time. "Can I get you a drink?" I ask her.

"Yes, please," she says, bringing her hand to her lips.

"Dru," my mother's voice drawls.

I turn to meet her gaze. "Hey Mom! Are you having fun?"

"I really am, Son. I'm enjoying watching you fall deeper in love with Charisse. I knew she was the one when you brought her to meet me that very first time. She's delightful, and she's so pretty. You two will give me such handsome grandsons." She puts one hand on her heart and uses the other to cup my face. "You took my order to heart, Dru, and I'm so proud of you. You're going to love being married."

She kisses my hand and walks away, leaving me feeling filthy. We need to get to the next part of the party right now.

I walk to the DJ booth and let him know it's time. He hands me the microphone.
"Charisse, my love. Where are you?" I look out over the crowd

and immediately spot her red dress.

"It's time for us to profess our love to each other in front of everyone." The crowd laughs.

Charisse throws her head back and laughs. It's good to see carefree and happy Charisse again. We've been in such an uncomfortable spot lately. I was nervous this party wouldn't be any fun, but it's warming my heart to watch her out there, dancing and enjoying herself.

She makes her way to the stage and snuggles up against me. The kiss she places on my cheek feels authentic and sadness ripples through me.

"Ladies first," I announce into the microphone before I hand it to her.

"Okay, but my speech is great, and you're going to have a really hard time topping it," she says with a sly smile.

"Dru Martin, who would have thought a little old teacher like me could end up with someone as fantastic as you? When I told my friends about you, one of them actually asked me if you were paying me to date you because we moved kind of fast and got smitten so quickly." She pauses, the crowd's laughter filling the room. It takes work, but I force my face into amusement. That was a slick move. She went all the way off script.

"As if, right? I don't think he could afford me if that were the case. I'm a damn good catch." More laughter fills the ballroom. "Anyway, to get serious, Dru, you've changed my outlook on so many things, but most of all on love. You showed me that I deserved to be showered in it, and you showed me it's safe to let my love out. I was so afraid to fall in love with you, but I couldn't help it. You all know how charismatic he is. I love the side of you only I get to see most, the laid back relaxed Dru. But all in all, I love every bit of you, and I can't wait to be your wife."

She moves in closer to me and hands me the microphone, then she sidles up to me and kisses me on my lips to the crowd's cheers. "Told you, you'd have a hard time topping that," she whispers in my ear.

"Hardly," I whisper back.

"I picked the right one. I knew it after our first date. The first real date, but I knew I had to get to know her better after she helped me fix my atrocious painting at the paint and sip we met at. Charisse was patient and helpful and full of energy, and she put me under her spell. I'd pay every last dime if I had to in order to keep you by my side. Luckily for my bank account, it just took me being myself. And dammit if that's not exactly what I crave most. Charisse is someone I can be my whole self around: no putting on airs, no business voice, no thinking through every single word I say. I can just exist around you. We can just exist together, and if that's not how life is supposed to be, then I know nothing. So, I'm more excited to spend the rest of my life being every bit of me with every bit of you. I love you, Charisse." I turn to her, and she's beaming. A simple head nod lets me know I did good.
I did better than good, and I'm about to show her.

The beautifully wrapped box I set in the front of the car earlier sits on a pedestal behind us on stage. I hand the microphone back to the DJ, telling him to get back to the music, and I walk her over to it.

"What is this? I didn't know gifts were involved. I didn't get you anything," she says.

I grin at her. "Gifts aren't standard, but I wanted to do something special for you. Open it." My heart pounds in my ears, and I have to put my hands in my pocket to hide how they sweat and tremble.

This is about to change everything, and I'm not ready for it at all.

She slowly pulls the ribbon at the top, painfully slow. My throat is dry, and I can hardly breathe. She finally gets the ribbon off. She looks up at me before she opens the box. I look anywhere but at her, taking slow, deep breaths.

"What's wrong with you?" she asks. Her hands hold the edges of the box, but she hasn't opened it yet.

"Nothing," I barely manage to say. "Open the box."

"If you say so," she tells me, more focused on me than the box.

"I'm nervous. I just want you to like your gift." It's true. I hope this brings her the joy she deserves.

"Your gifts are always wonderful. You're the best gift giver I've ever met. What makes this different?"

I'm going to die right here if she doesn't just open the damn box. "Open it," I croak. I need a drink.

"Fine, but you can admit that you're being weird."

I nod and wave my hand at the box. She's looking at me as she opens it. I want to scream. Instead, I plaster a smile on my face and wait the eternity it takes for her to look down.

She pulls up a handful of shredded paper and laughs. "Did you get me confetti? The nerves make sense now because this is not what I was expecting."

"Look closer," I tell her.

She holds the handful of shredded paper up to her face. "Void? I think I can make out the word 'void' on these." She studies them more, pulling single strands out. "Is this?" She drops the paper strips back into the box and brings her hands to her mouth.

"You voided the contract?" she whispers, tears now streaming down her face.

"I did. Everything you said was valid, and it's true that I met my dream girl and put her under contract. I trapped you into this for my own selfish reasons, and the goodness in you realized it's not the right way to do this," I tell her.

"What about...everything?" she asks me, holding back her sobs.

"I'll figure it out. And you can keep everything you got from our time together. No harm, no foul. They're all gifts to you."

"Dru, I can't." She's sobbing now, but trying to keep it together.

"What would Porsche do?" I ask her, chuckling.

This gets a laugh out of her. "Porsche would keep it all and try to calculate how much you owed her up until today."

I scan the crowd for Porsche, and she's at the bar with two drinks. I laugh and pull Charisse into a hug.

"I meant every word I said up here today though. And I wish our circumstances had been different. We're pretty perfect together."

Chapter 31

Charisse

"He voided it!?" Porsche screams. She and Lily are on my couch, dressed in their Puerto Rico pajamas. Dru has left his imprint everywhere in my life.

"And you can keep all the money, the rings, the clothes, everything?" She screams again. She's so drunk; it's beyond funny.

I nod.

"He really loves you," Lily proclaims quietly.

"And bitch, if you didn't love him before, you better now!" Porsche adds, falling back onto the couch with her eyes closed. "You love him though. I see it"

This sleepover tonight was a bad idea. I didn't think the night would turn out the way it did. All I want to do is sit on my bed and process everything that's happened, But I'm stuck here with the drunken one and the therapist who are going to want to talk this out all night long.

"I'm tired." I sigh. It's trueish, but I really just want to be alone. I head to my room and close the door and lay on my bed, staring at the ceiling.

I wait until I know they're asleep, which only takes about thirty minutes because they're both absolutely drunk and exhausted from the day, then I slip out my front door. I need to take a drive.

I'm more worried about the repercussions facing Dru than I am about the fact that I'm now free. He's not going to be able to get what he wants. And he gave that up to make me happy. I didn't think this deal through at all, and now every move I make fills me with regret. I hate this more than the idea of lying to my family, who I'm just now realizing never made the effort to show up tonight.

Subconsciously, I knew where I was headed the moment I left my house. Seeing Dru's car parked in the lot to his workshop makes my heart clench. I park and head to the door with no plan at all. I just need to see him.

I knock on the door as I open it. He has on his goggles and he's sanding something. "Knock knock!" I yell, hoping he hears me over the sander.

He looks up in surprise, a smile taking over his face as he realizes it's me.

"Hey!" he says and takes off his protective gear. "What brings you here?"

"I don't know," I confess. I just felt drawn here, but that's a very Lily thing to say.

"Well, I'm happy to see you. How'd your girls react to the news?" He wipes sweat off his brow and beams at me.

"Porsche was excited, duh. Lily's more stoic." I shrug.

"How are you reacting, now that there's no audience?"

That's what I'm here trying to figure out. How am I reacting to everything between us being over?

"I'm not as happy as I should be, if I'm being honest." I look up from where I'd been staring at my feet.

He cocks his head to the side and studies me, opening his mouth to say something, then closing it. He steps closer to me, dusting himself off.

"Why is that?" he asks when he's in my airspace. My breath hitches, and any words I had disappear.

He lifts my chin with his forefinger, forcing me to look into his eyes. "Why is that?" he repeats.

"Because I'm in love with you." It just comes out, but now that it's in the universe, it feels right. I don't know how long I've been in love with him, but the feeling overwhelms me now. A laugh bubbles out of me. That's why this didn't feel right. I've been faking what's been real this whole time. We worked to get to know each other to make everything look real, and what we really did was make it real.

"Finally. Fucking finally!" he exclaims as he grabs me around my waist and swings me in the air. He sets me down carefully, then he gets down on one knee.

"What are you doing?" I squeal.

He takes my hand. "I'm doing it right. I really want to marry you and build a real future with you, have babies with you, and be myself forever with you. Charisse Turner, will you really marry me?"

I kneel down with him and take his face into my hands. "Of

course I will marry you, Dru," I tell him before we kiss.

Epilogue

The morning sun kisses the garden, turning everything it touches into gold. I stand at the entrance, my heart fluttering like the delicate wings of the butterflies flitting around the blooming flowers. Everyone I love stands at the end of the aisle. Today, in front of the world, I marry Dru, the man who turned my world upside down, in the best way possible.

I smooth down my dress, a sleek, modern creation that feels like a second skin. It's perfect—just like this day promises to be. Porsche and Lily stand looking like beauty queens. I had no involvement in their dress buying. Dru put them on a plane with an unlimited budget, and they absolutely understood the assignment.

Taking a deep breath, I step forward into the next chapter of my life. My gaze locks on Dru. He stands at the altar, looking like he stepped out of a dream, in his custom suit with a razor sharp hairline. His eyes brim with emotions. This has been an interesting journey. It's hard to believe we've made it.

As I walk down the aisle, I catch glimpses of our friends and family. Draymond and Drummond are here, their twin presence a comforting reminder of the bond Dru shares with them. They're laughing about something, their heads close together —a moment I know Dru will cherish. I hope one of the photographers catches that.

Porsche and Lily are side by side with Dreya, ever the picture of sophistication, standing beside them. My relationship with my sister may still be broken, but these three women are my chosen family.

Reaching the altar, Dru takes my hands in his, and his touch sends a wave of warmth through me. "You look stunning," he whispers, and I can only smile in response.

Everything is a blur until Dru begins his vows. His hands are warm and steady, a testament to how he feels about what we're doing. There's not a nervous bone in his body right now.

"Charisse, from the moment I met you, my world shifted on its axis. You came into my life like a whirlwind, challenging me, inspiring me, and showing me what it truly means to love and be loved. Today, as I stand before you, I am overwhelmed with gratitude and love.

"In your eyes, I see a future filled with laughter, passion, and endless possibilities. In your smile, I find the warmth and comfort of home. And in your heart, I've discovered a love so profound, it transcends everything I ever imagined.

"I vow to be your partner in every sense of the word. To stand by you through the highs and the lows, the triumphs and the challenges. I promise to listen to you, to learn from you, and to grow with you, day by day.

"I vow to cherish the quirks that make you uniquely you, to celebrate your strengths, and to offer my shoulder for the moments when you feel weak. I will be your confidant, your co-conspirator, and your closest friend.

"I promise to keep our lives exciting, adventurous, and full of passion. To support your dreams and to walk beside you as we build our future together.

"And above all, I vow to be true to you, to respect you, and to shower you with all the love I have, for all the days of my life.

"Charisse, you are my heart, my soul, my everything. Today, I give you my hand, my heart, and my promise, that no matter where life takes us, I will always be there, loving you more and more with each passing day."

I'm fighting back tears, and I take a shaky breath before I say my own.

"Dru, when I first met you, I never imagined that this day would come. Our beginning was like a dance, one where I was convinced I knew all the steps, yet you came along and changed the rhythm entirely. My friends saw it before I did — they saw how you'd come to mean the world to me. And me? I spent far too long denying the truth that was as clear as day: I had fallen for you, completely and irrevocably.

"I vow to be your partner, your confidante, your pillar of strength in every challenge we face. In you, I've found a love that is both a sanctuary and a spark, a love that inspires and comforts.

"I promise to cherish every moment with you, from the quiet mornings to the starry nights. To stand beside you, to dream with you, and to build a future that's brighter because we're together.

"I vow to keep our love alive, to nurture it with kindness, understanding, and patience. To remember that even on the difficult days, what we have is rare and beautiful.

"I promise to listen to you with an open heart, to speak words of love and encouragement, and to always be the one you can lean on. My love for you is a journey, starting at forever and ending at never.

"Dru, you are my unexpected love, my greatest adventure, and my eternal comfort. Today, in front of our families, our friends who knew all along, and the world, I give you my hand, my heart, and my promise. A promise to love you more deeply with each passing day, in every chapter of the beautiful story we are writing together."

We seal our vows with a kiss. We'd agreed on a little peck, but Dru takes my face into his hands and brings his lips to mine like I'm water, and he's a man lost at sea. He drinks me in, caressing my cheek as his tongue glides across mine. He bites my bottom lip, making me moan quietly.

"They're watching," I say into Dru's mouth as he extends the kiss for much longer than anticipated. "You're going to make me want to leave before we get to the reception."

He pulls away. "You're my wife now. We're going to do what husbands and wives do—right now, and definitely later." He kisses me again and grabs my ass, causing the crowd to erupt in cheers and applause.

The reception is a whirlwind of music, laughter, and dancing. I find myself swept into conversations with everyone, feeling like the happiest person alive.

Porsche scoffs at me after catching the bouquet. "You set this up. I don't want this!" she teases, her laugh infectious. She holds the bouquet to her heart and dances with it. Lily stands beside her laughing.

Draymond and Drummond stand at the microphone to give the Best Man's toast. Dru hangs his head knowing the nonsense they're about to spew. I nudge him and smile. His brothers love him so much.

"Dru," Draymond begins, "How did you manage to pull someone like Charisse?"

"He flashed his money because we know he has no game," Draymond answers, making Dru's face fall.

I stand up and feign offense with my hands on my hips at the idea of being bought, then I glance at Dru and wink. This is going to be our inside joke throughout our whole marriage. The crowd roars with laughter, and eventually Dru joins in.

"But for real, Dru, we love you and we're happy for you. Charisse, we come as a package deal, so it's nice to have two sisters now. You fit in and match the energy so well. We're happy to have you in the family," Draymond finishes.

I stand up and blow kisses at both of them, mouthing "Thank you" and putting my hand to my heart. I'm joining a family that embraces me completely, and it's everything I never knew I needed.

Dru and I steal a moment together over our meal, our fingers entwined. "We did it," he says, his voice thick with emotion.

"We did," I agree, leaning into him. "We can keep this contract signed though."

He bursts out laughing and holds his drink up to me. "We can definitely drink to that!"

As the night draws to a close, Dru and I share our final dance under the stars. The world falls away until it's just the two of us, moving to a rhythm that's ours alone.

"We're starting a new chapter," I say, my head resting on his shoulder and imagining the life I never thought I'd have with the love I didn't think I deserved.

"A beautiful, endless chapter," Dru agrees, and I know he's right.

The End

Books In This Series

The Martin Brothers

Dru, Draymond, and Drummond Martin have the money, the looks, and the swag, but they don't have the women who make their lives complete.

Love, Under Contract

Love, From Scratch

Coming in April!

Love, Undercover

Made in the USA
Monee, IL
21 July 2024

62191954R00138